OF ALL THE PLACES I'VE FALLEN

I'VE FALLEN

S. E. Walker

ISBN-13: 979-8-9936729-1-5

Cover Art by S. E. Walker
Library of Congress Control Number: 2018675309
Printed in the United States of America

Dedicated to dear Scotland, the first and last love of my life.

TRIGGER WARNING

This may be a story about finding love, but just like real life, it's also a story about trauma and
healing. So many people have gone through abuse in their lives, myself included. I understand how
reading something that is in any way similar to something you've experienced can be a trigger. Because I
love my readers, you need to know that before you start this story, it contains the following themes:

Domestic abuse
Sexual assault
Physical violence
Knives

Also, this is a story about romance, which means that there are scenes depicting intimacy in detail.
If you're not a fan of spicy romance, then this may not be the book for you. But I wanted to show that a
story about romance and sex could be passionate and powerful without relying on fear, pain, or a
dominant/submissive dynamic. These scenes are built from tenderness and love, protection and
understanding, healing and hope.

I hope that they resonate with you, my friends.

S.E. Walker

CONTENTS

SARAH

My company transferred me from Philly to our newly expanded international office in Inverness almost 8 months ago. Yet, during that time, all I had managed to do was fall into a dull, cyclical routine of work, eat, sleep, repeat. What made my situation even more depressing was that four days a week, I worked remotely from my flat. It was only on Fridays that I made an in-person appearance at the office for meetings, training sessions, and "team building," whatever that actually meant. My only non-work-related outings had been to the local market for the occasional grocery run, and once to the local Tesco's for new deodorant and toothpaste. Yeah, I know, I live such an exciting life. I can tell that you're just green with envy.

I'm not sure what inspired me to pluck up the courage and join my coworkers at the pub a block from the office one Friday after work. I'm really not much of a drinker. One or two, and I'm good for a few months. But Aislin and Cara had promised that I would have a good time, so there I was, sitting at the bar nursing a whiskey and coke, watching the two women drunkenly sing "What's Up" by 4 Non-Blondes as their current choice for karaoke. They waved at me from the stage and I raised my glass in a toast to their off-key yet enthusiastic performance.

"What am I doing here?" I wondered for the 17th time in the last hour. This really wasn't my scene. Not that I minded the pub, it was nice enough. People were laughing and having a good time. I liked having a good time, didn't I? I was fun! I sighed. I couldn't even convince myself of that in my own inner dialogue. I had to face facts: I was a dull, nerdy, bordering on old-aged woman whose idea of the perfect night was a pizza, a fuzzy blanket, and a Lord of the Rings marathon—the extended editions, of course.

You would think that living in my dream country, I would find myself exploring and seeing the countryside. I had always wanted to see Scotland; it was top of my travel bucket list and had been since I was a child. A lonely childhood dreaming of worldwide adventures had morphed into a lonely adulthood, complete with a failed seven-year marriage, years of struggle,

3

abuse, and financial pain, which, of course, eliminated any thoughts of travel. At the ripe old age of 39, I had finally landed a job that I wouldn't exactly call a dream, but it was comfortably boring with a hefty paycheck and a wonderfully quiet lack of dealing with the general public. After years of retail sales jobs, a desk job from home was as close as a "dream" as I could get! After my one-year anniversary with my company, the opportunity came along for the Inverness office, and I couldn't pass it up. I was painfully single, renting an apartment in a shady neighborhood with weekly shootings and fights in the parking lot. A chance to live in Scotland AND still work from home? Yes please! So I sold my furniture and my car, put a few things into storage, packed up my clothes, books, and a few knick-knacks I couldn't part with, and hopped on a plane.

My new flat was small but adorable. One bedroom was all I needed. I had a decent view of the city from my living room, and on Fridays, my office was only a ten-minute walk away. The first week, I made lists of places I wanted to visit, planning grand weekend trips in my mind. After the first month of not leaving the neighborhood, the travel plans waned. By the second month, I was in a comfortable routine, and thoughts of adventures seemed so distant. I was content to just enjoy my time at home, boring and quiet. Hey, at least I was in Scotland, right?

The song ended, and Aislin stumbled over to me, grinning wickedly. "Ok, Sarah, it's your turn!"

Startled, I raised my eyebrows at her. "Pardon? I don't think so!"

Her laugh sprinkled the air with glitter as she grabbed my hand. "Aye, I already signed you up! You can't say no now!"

"Wait, what?? What song? I don't know about this, Aislin!" I tried to protest, desperately looking for a place to disappear. I hadn't sung in front of people since my teenage years in church. What was she thinking?

Cara joined us and waved down the bartender for another round. "Did you tell her she's up now?"

Aislin giggled again, her blonde hair flowing like an ethereal elf. "I did, but I don't think she believes me."

I looked at them, still wondering why they even invited me. They were both in their early 30s, beautiful and outgoing. Aislin had a petite build, stunning blue eyes, and a smile that caught the attention of every single man within a 20 km radius like a homing beacon. Cara was built like an athlete, a perfect gymnast's body, and had short, buzzed black hair with the exception of a bright fire-engine red faux-hawk that always looked perfect. She had stunning tattoo sleeves on both arms, a piercing in both eyebrows, her nose, and her lip. I had been told in a few other places that I wasn't shown due to them not being office-appropriate. They both radiated confidence and charm, which was incredibly disconcerting when looking at myself in comparison.

For being almost 41, I've been told that I didn't exactly look my age. Most people say I could pass for early to mid-thirties, but I think they're being generous. After my life experiences, I'm lucky I didn't look seventy! I was short, curvy, a bit of a belly that hung over my waistband (although I was good at hiding that), and mousy shoulder-length hair that was somewhere between brown and blonde with none of the natural highlights that would have made it look bright and lively. My favorite feature was my eyes. They were a hazel color that shifted to blues, greens, or grays depending on what I was wearing or what the weather was on that particular day. I have to admit that I loved my eyes, but they were always partially hidden by my cat-eye glasses. If I bothered to wear makeup, a little mascara would make them really pop, but I didn't usually put in the time to mess with it. I had a small level of fashion sense, but mostly dressed for comfort at home, and since I didn't get out much, there wasn't much variety. When I agreed to go out with the girls that night, I rummaged through my closet to find a pair of jeans and a black lacy shirt that actually looked fairly flattering when I combined it with my best black push-up bra. Adding in my silver and turquoise bracelet and matching necklace, it was the best I'd looked in years!

Giving Aislin a withering glare, I continued my protest. "I don't want to sing, I can't get up there in front of people!"

She waved my comment away. "No one is actually paying attention. And I know you can sing. I've heard you at the office Christmas party when we were all singing carols. You've got a great voice! But even if you didn't, karaoke is about having fun, not how talented people are! Come on, I picked a great song for you. It's one I know you like. I've seen it on your playlist!"

Considering my wide variety of musical tastes, that didn't exactly comfort me. "What song?"

She flashed me another dazzling smile. "Criminal by Fiona Apple!"

I paused and took a breath. That was actually a song that I could probably pull off, if I had the guts to actually get up on the stage. Glancing around the pub, I assessed the crowd. The late winter rain was pelting the windows, but that hadn't stopped people from making their way to their favorite hangout. The tables were mostly full with joyful people chatting and laughing. But, they weren't really paying much attention to the few people that had been on the stage, so... maybe?

Cara grinned and handed me a shot glass. "Come on, gal. Throw back this shot and go for it! If you crash and burn, it's not like you come here often. What have you got to lose?"

Somehow that actually made me feel better. She was right, the chances of me coming back to the pub were slim to none. So if I made a fool of myself, what did it matter? I wanted to get out and do things like a normal person. Normal people sing karaoke, don't they? I took the shot, stared at it for a second, wondering what was in it, then decided I didn't care and downed it. Whatever it was burned satisfyingly, and I slammed it upside down on the bar, which is what I assumed people do when they've finished a shot (I'm sure I've seen that in the movies).

"Ok, let's do this!" I tried to calm the butterflies in my stomach, and I wound my way through the tables on the way to the small stage in the corner. Most nights, there were local bands playing, but every third Friday night, the stage was reserved for the karaoke event. I suppose it was my luck that the night I was talked into leaving the comfort of my flat just so happened to be one of those Fridays.

"The universe is trying to tell you something, love." I could hear my mom's voice in my head. Easy for her to say; she'd had a fantastic singing voice. I used to love singing along with her rich alto harmonies, but it was always her voice that truly carried the tune. I remembered how much she enjoyed humming along to Fiona Apple on the car radio, and that gave me some comfort.

I took the microphone off the stand, and Cara gave the DJ a nod. He flashed me a huge grin and addressed the crowd, his English accent sounding a bit out of place.

"We have a new singer for you all tonight! Singing Criminal, it's..." He glanced down at his sign-up sheet. "Sarah Calvin! Let's give 'er a big hand!"

A weak applause sounded around the room from the people who were actually listening, which thankfully wasn't many. I smiled shakily and waited for the music to start. At the first few notes of the familiar song, I closed my eyes. I didn't need to follow the lyrics on the screen. This was a song I knew by heart. How many times had I sung this in the car? Or in the shower? When I was alone, I could belt this out and hit every note perfectly, and I knew that. So maybe if I didn't look at the faces staring up at me, I could pretend I was alone, standing in my living room with the YouTube video playing. When my cue hit, I began softly.

"I've been a bad, bad girl... I've been careless with a delicate maaaan... And it's a sad, sad wooorrrlldd... when a girl will break a boy just because she caaaan!"

Getting through that first line without my voice cracking gave my confidence a boost, and I got bolder, louder.

"Don't you tell me to deny it. I've done wrong, and I want to suffer for my sins."

I didn't open my eyes for the next several lines, not until after the chorus when I fell into a groove and had the guts to look over at Cara and Aislin as I started the second verse.

"*Heaven help me for the waaaay I am, save me from these evil deeds before I get them done...*"   And I immediately made eye contact with the most gorgeous man I'd ever seen. I almost forgot the words as he gave me a sly smile. He towered over Cara, who had her arm linked with his, his stance relaxed as he leaned against the bar, watching me. He had broad shoulders, thick biceps, and the build of a true weightlifter, almost barrel-chested with enough cushion around his waist that I automatically knew he would be amazing at cuddling. He was dressed in a gray button-up shirt and vest, jeans, and heavy-looking black boots. His reddish blonde beard was long but neatly groomed, and under his flat cap, it looked like his head was shaved. His rolled-up shirt sleeves showed off a myriad of tattoos. It was as if some AI machine had taken the keywords "perfect Scottish biker hunk" and spat him out.

I managed to only miss one beat before I caught myself. "*Tomorrow brings the consequence at hand, but I keep living this day like the next will never coooooome.*"

He winked at me when I sang that last word. My knees almost buckled. Cara stretched up to whisper something in his ear, and he broke eye contact with me, which made me remember that I needed to breathe.

"*Oh help me but don't tell me to deennyyyy iiiit...*"

It was a good thing that I had these lyrics committed to memory because my mind was spinning. He is gorgeous! Of course, he's with Cara; they look like a good match. Lucky bitch. Just how tall is he?? I wonder what those tattoos are?

"*I've got to cleanse myself of all these lies 'til I'm good enough for hiiiim...*"

He looked back up at me and winked again.

"*I've got a lot to lose and I'm bettin' high so I'm begging you, before it ends just tell me where to begin...*"

Cara motioned to an empty table closer to the stage, then over to Aislin, and the mystery man nodded. The three of them grabbed their drinks and moved over to the table. He took the seat closest to me as I started the chorus again.

"What I neeeeed is a good defense, 'cause I'm feeeeeling like a criminaaal and I need to be redeemed to the one I've sinned against because he's all I ever kneeew of loo-oo-oove."

He never looked away from me as I repeated the chorus for the last time. I completely forgot that there were any other people in the pub; all I saw were his green eyes (now that he was closer, I could see how beautifully green they were) and how they had a sexy, mischievous glint.

"Because he's all I ever knew of looo-ooo-oooove!" The last few notes of the song slowly faded away, and for a split second (which to me felt like an eternity), there was deadly silence. Then suddenly everyone began to applaud. Not just clapping, but whistles and cheers, even some stomping. Mystery Guy joined in, standing up and smiling at me as he clapped. Who was this guy??

I smiled shyly at the room, nodded over to the DJ, and put the mic back on the stand, my face flushing. Aislin grabbed my hand and pulled me into the empty chair at their table.

"I told you! You were fantastic!!" She gave me another shot, I'm assuming to help calm my nerves. "You have to come back and do this again. You've brought the house down!"

"Aye, tha's the best voice this pub has heard in a long time!" The deep voice caught me off guard. I looked over at the man sitting at our table. Close up, he was even more beautiful than before. I saw a braid hanging down his back, and I realized that only the sides of his head were shaved. I wondered what he looked like without that flat cap. I pinched my leg to break his spell and reminded myself that he was here with Cara.

"Thanks," I stuttered. "I wasn't sure I could do it."

Cara laughed, "Well, now you know better. We'll have to make a monthly date to come here for you to sing for your fans!" There were a few people calling for an encore from the other side of the room. "Ah, Sarah, this is Liam, my big brother. He lives in Drumnadrochit, but I talked him into coming to the city tonight to meet up with us!"

My breath caught in my chest. Brother? I looked closer and

suddenly saw the similar features, the same smile. "Oh, um, hi, nice to meet you!"

He winked again (what was with this guy? Did he have a twitch? Or did he really just flirt that much?) "Nice to meet you too, Princess."

I frowned. "Princess?" I didn't like pet names from people I just met; it rubbed me the wrong way.

"Aye, that's what your name means, right? Princess."

I blushed, "Oh, yeah... it does." The meaning of my name had always made me feel awkward. It felt conceited, like I thought too much of myself.

Liam grinned, "Well... are you?"

I looked up at him sharply. "Am I what?"

"A princess. You're beautiful, have the voice of an angel, so you must be a princess. But, based on that song, I'd say definitely not of the Disney variety." He raised his eyebrow approvingly. "I bet you've got a dirty, dark personality hidden under that librarian facade."

At the bright redness suddenly flowing through my cheeks, he laughed while the girls joined in, and I wanted to melt into my chair. Who did he think he was? The arrogance, he didn't know anything about me. It didn't matter that he was right and was reading me like a book. My exasperation was more out of embarrassment than anger, but I had spent years building up walls to protect myself, and I didn't like feeling so vulnerable under his gaze.

I excused myself to go get another drink from the bar, mostly just to catch my breath and recover from him. I told the bartender I wanted another shot of whatever Cara had given me earlier, and as soon as I tossed it back, I felt a warm presence behind me.

Liam was looking down at me, and god help me, he was gorgeous! His expression didn't match his arrogant countenance. In fact, there was something in his eyes that looked nervous or, dare I say, shy?

Then he opened his mouth.

"So, I hear that you are quite the wild woman."

I raised my eyebrow suspiciously. "Oh, is that right?"

He nodded and motioned for another round. "Aye. I've heard some stories, you dirty Princess, you. You like how you're into orgies and such. That you like it ropes and…" he paused as if his brain was computing how to say his next sentence. "That you like it rough." His last words were said almost in a whisper, so quiet and deep I felt it low in my stomach.

I was speechless, a thousand thoughts spinning around in my mind. First, what the hell had Cara told him? Second, the fucking balls of this man to just start a conversation like that! Also, he's so beautiful, I honestly wouldn't mind if he threw me over his shoulder... no, what I meant was... who the fuck does he think he is?

"Is this bloke botherin' ya, darlin'?"

I turned to see the DJ standing a little too close for comfort, giving Liam the evil eye. The DJ tried to put his arm around my shoulder, but I ducked away, giving him a weak smile.

"No, it's fine, thanks."

Liam seemed to grow taller beside me, his shoulders expanding into a mountain as he stared down at the skinny DJ. Was... was he being protective? Possessive? I couldn't tell which, and I also couldn't tell if I was annoyed or turned on. Honestly, I think it was both.

The DJ withered a bit under Liam's steely gaze. He raised his glass of beer at me and began backing away. "Well, you just let me know if you need some help." With that, he walked over to apparently flirt with the women at the table near the end of the bar.

Turning back to Liam, I frowned. "Listen, I don't know what you've heard…"

"Only that I should bring my A-game before I get involved with you, Princess," he interjected.

"First of all, who says you're going to get involved with me? Second, just because my name means 'princess' doesn't mean I want to be called that by YOU!"

He laughed, but something about it didn't quite reach his eyes. If I didn't know better, I'd say he looked scared. "Well, when a name means something so accurate, it'd be a shame not to use it."

"And what does Liam mean? Bully? Ignorant? Or maybe just Fucking Asshole?"

His eyes darkened to an amazingly deep green, like the sea during a summer thunderstorm. And while the smile never left his face, it tightened, and his posture stiffened.

Surprised at my own outburst and embarrassed for several different reasons, I turned and walked back to Cara and Aislin. "Thanks for the fun night, girls. I really need to get going. I have to get up early in the morning." A complete lie. I just needed to get out of there.

Before anyone could say another word, I grabbed my coat and practically ran out the door into the rain. I didn't bother trying to find a taxi since my flat was only a few blocks away. Maybe the rain would help cool down the flush I felt from what I had said and from how alarmingly hot Liam was.

Why had I said that? It wasn't as though he was wrong, and with anyone else I probably would have bantered back with some sly quip about keeping handcuffs in my purse or something. I'm not shy about things like that. The girls at work were always shocked to hear my stories from the past, my experimental stage, my kinky phase that was more at the insistence of my partner at the time, my years of acting like a sub at my dom's bidding. I had convinced myself I enjoyed that lifestyle, the threesomes and random guys. Sure, I had a wild past, but that was when I was in my twenties. I'm an old lady now! The idea of all those things just sounded exhausting now, plus they triggered memories of a time when I had no choice in the matter.

Don't get me wrong, I still wanted to find someone who could put me against the wall and kiss me while his hand was around my throat, ahem... I mean. What girl doesn't want the book-like romance of a man who acts possessive and throws you

LIAM

The cold rain almost made him change his mind about meeting his little sister at the pub, but he had promised. He hated disappointing Cara; she was eleven years younger and had him wrapped around her little finger from the day she was born. When she had asked him about joining her and her friends that night, he had been suspicious, as it wouldn't have been the first time she had tried hooking him up with someone. In fact, this would be the sixth attempt if his memory served him right. Each time, Cara would ensure him that this would be "the one" and that his search for love was over. He didn't realize he was searching for love, but apparently his sister was doing all the searching for him. It had been 9 years since his divorce from Fiona, and he had been quite content alone since then, preferring solitude to the possibility of being cheated on and getting his heart broken once again. But Cara had a way of persuading him to do whatever she asked and he would find himself at dinners with dreadfully dull or impossibly crazy women almost half his age and he would suffer through the evenings just long enough to satisfy his sister that he at least made an attempt, then he would slip away without taking the phone numbers these women offered in hopes of a second date.

"Not another one, Car, I really don't feel like it." He groaned when she had called.

"Liam, trust me, this time is different!" She protested.

Liam shook his head and laughed, "You say that every time!"

"I mean it! I've never introduced you to someone like this. First, she's about your age! I work with her and she's got this nerdy thing going on. But trust me, this chick's a freak once you get to know her. She's always telling the most insane stories about her life and the things she's done. I'm telling ya, she's kinky and the good kind of crazy, just the way you like 'em!"

Doubtful but intrigued, Liam sighed. "All right, love. I'll be there."

Cara squealed just like she had since she was a little girl, the sound melting his heart as always. He couldn't say no to her. At least this time, she had said Sarah was somewhat close to his age.

He had just celebrated his 44th birthday last month, and Cara had promised him that she would find him a woman. No matter how much he tried to convince her that it wasn't necessary, she had just waved his comments away, saying she knew him better and he needed someone in his life. He didn't bother to remind her of what happened with his last relationship.

Fiona had been the fiery whirlwind that turned his world upside down, a three-month relationship before he had proposed, then just a two-month engagement ending in a courthouse wedding, followed by five years of fights, screaming, and dodging the random plates or knives that she threw his way. He could fully admit that he was not innocent; he would find himself yelling back at her, but the one rule he stood firmly on was that he never got physical with her. He'd watched his father do that with his mother and swore from a young age that he would never lay a hand on a woman in anger. Fiona, on the other hand, would slap, kick, punch, whatever she could do to try and push his buttons and make him lash out. He realized that she was trying to make him react in kind so that she could turn the situation against him and claim domestic abuse. After he caught her cheating for the third time, he had learned that she was always telling people that the men in her life beat her, and she would play the victim to anyone who would listen.

When he finally realized she was never going to change, he made the decision to file for divorce. She tried to claim that he hit her in court, but she hadn't realized he put a camera in their front lounge and had recorded the night in question, the footage showing clearly that he had stood silently while she ranted and ran at him with a kitchen knife. The judge had offered for him to press charges of his own, but he had just asked for the divorce and an order of protection to keep her as far away as possible. He didn't need to send her to jail; he just wanted to be free and find a way to mend his broken heart.

Now he spent his days working at his shop repairing classic cars and motorcycles, and taking his own bike around the country on scenic trips to clear his mind. He didn't mind the solitude, it was peaceful and didn't have the risk of being hurt.

When he pulled up to the pub that Friday night, he was already prepared to leave after 30 minutes or so, despite Cara's insistence that Sarah was exactly what he was looking for. He spotted his sister and her friend Aislin as soon as he walked in, by the bar, watching the stage with ridiculously happy grins on their faces. He followed their gaze and stopped in his tracks.

Under the spotlight on the stage was a beautiful woman, her eyes closed, gripping the mic like it was the only thing keeping her from disappearing. The notes of the song flowed over him, one of his favorite 90s female vocalists, and this frightened woman on the stage had a voice that pierced his heart. She looked petite yet curvy in all the right places from the way her jeans fit over her hips. The lace of her black shirt showed off her amazing cleavage, and he was so focused on watching her that he almost jumped out of his skin when Cara grabbed his arm and reached up to kiss his cheek.

"I'm so glad you're here, Li!" She smiled as she pulled him over to the spot at the bar where Aislin waited. "I thought you were going to blow me off tonight."

He gave his sister a sly grin. "I almost did. You know how these things go."

She shrugged and said, "Usually, sure. But this time is different. See?" and she pointed at the stage.

"That... that's her?" Liam stared at the beauty singing, her eyes still closed. He could tell she was feeling every word of the song. This couldn't be the woman his sister was trying to set him up with? The freaky woman with wild stories who, according to Cara, wanted to find some kinky guy for wild adventures. This woman looked more like a gothic angel in that black lace shirt and tight jeans tucked into tall black boots. He realized that he was smiling like a fool as he stared when Sarah opened her eyes and met his gaze. He couldn't help but wink at her when she sang the line *but I keep living this day like the next will never coooome!*"

"That's her! You should hear the stories she tells us girls at work. She's wicked for sure!" Cara and Aislin laughed.

When Cara said they were going to grab a table closer to the stage, he didn't argue. A chance for a closer look sounded good to him. Her voice was mesmerizing, not to mention he was blown away by how gorgeous she was. Maybe not in a traditional way. She was a thicker build, and she wore no makeup that he could see. But in his opinion, that natural beauty was stunning, and he was finding himself wanting to talk to her, wanting to learn everything about this woman whose singing was pulling him in like a siren.

Remembering what his sister had told him about Sarah, he suddenly felt nervous. Was she really as wild and crazy as that? He wasn't sure he could handle crazy again. But maybe she was just one of those women who loved to flirt. He was going to have to really step up his game to make a good first impression. If she liked wicked flirting, he was going to give her exactly what she liked.

To be honest, he didn't really remember exactly what he said to her when he followed her to the bar. He had pulled some flirtatious words out of the back of his memory, something he was sure he had heard in a film once. But as soon as he said them, he saw her face darken.

"And what does Liam mean? Bully? Ignorant? Or maybe just Asshole?"

Immediately embarrassed, he found himself blushing and regretting his words. But he also darkened at being called ignorant. That was Fiona's favorite insult, throwing it in his face that he hadn't been able to get through university due to his severe dyslexia and ADHD. The fact that he pushed himself and got through trade school later for mechanics didn't matter; he was just a dumb dropout in her eyes, and she never let him forget it. Hearing Sarah say that hit a part of his soul that he thought he had walled off and immediately triggered memories of past screaming matches with his ex. He found he wasn't upset when Sarah made up an excuse and ran out of the pub, at least not at first. Then he thought back over the conversation and felt guilt pierce his heart. He had pushed it too far. That's not how to start talking to a woman like her, not when he wanted to actually get to know her. He should have known better than to listen to Cara and her interpretation of Sarah's personality.

Then there was that scrawny DJ, trying to put his arm around Sarah like he was saving her from the conversation. Liam couldn't explain why that had angered him so much, but there was something about that guy that made Liam's skin crawl. He had been so pleased to see Sarah pull away from that asshole and make it clear she didn't want his help.

Sighing, he took his almost empty lager and went back to the table with the girls.

"Well, that's not what I expected," Cara huffed.

"Me either," replied Aislin, finishing her ale. "I wonder what crawled up her ass?"

Liam shook his head. "I shouldn't have said that."

Cara waved his comment away, "Naw, she just took it the wrong way." She motioned to the waitress for another round, her frown making her disappointment obvious. "She's more stuck up than I thought, I guess."

No, she's not stuck up; she's just softer than she lets on. Liam thought, distracting himself by draining the last of his lager. Before the waitress could bring him another, he stood.

"I appreciate the invite, little sis, but I'm going home. I'll give you a call later this week." And before she could respond, he was out the door and getting into his car. His mind was a battle of feeling guilty over the things he had said and feeling angry at the things she had said. Why did it matter to him? She was a total stranger to him; he shouldn't be this upset. Her opinion shouldn't affect him in the slightest.

But as he drove home, he realized that it was affecting him. And the flash in her eyes, a mix of embarrassment, shame, and anger, was etched into his mind. He found himself trying to think of a way he could make it up to her, that is, if he ever got the chance to see her again.

SARAH

Over the next few weeks, I managed to successfully avoid Cara at the office. It was too awkward, and I just didn't know how to approach the subject. I was ashamed of what I had said, but I was also still bristling at the things Liam had said to me. I think I was also just confused.

What exactly did I want from a man? I liked the thought of someone flirting with me, didn't I? Yes, that sounded fun. But how often had flirting quickly turned into assumptions that I would shag any man who showed the slightest interest? Like, the only value in starting a conversation with me was that it would result in sex. I had so much more to offer. It wasn't that I didn't like sex; trust me, I did. But the idea of empty, meaningless sex just didn't appeal to me now. I had outgrown the desire for something casual and found that what I craved was something deeper, something intimate and soulful. When that proved difficult to find, I had resolved myself to be alone, not to settle for anything less. It was better to be alone and confident than to find herself in a relationship that was draining and surface-level.

Still, should I apologize to Liam for my comments and running out of the pub like that? Part of me kept thinking about how that apology would go, but every imaginary scenario I played out ended badly, in more rejection. No, it was better to just keep living my life and pretend like that night never happened. He was probably a jerk anyway. Guys who are good-looking usually are conceited and think every woman wants them. It was probably just a waste of time to think about trying to make it up to him.

When a bouquet of roses was delivered to my doorstep, my first thought was maybe they were from Liam! Don't be stupid, he's not given you another thought after all this time. It's been a month!

I thanked the delivery guy and carried the flowers into my kitchen, searching for a card. There was a small note buried in the center, "To my 'criminal', love, your biggest fan."

What the fuck?

I had no idea who these could be from. I seriously didn't

think Liam had sent these; he wasn't a fan of mine for sure. Maybe someone had just liked my singing that night? But how did they know where I lived? No one at the pub knew me. Suddenly feeling unsettled, I decided to throw the flowers out. When there was another knock at the door the next day with a delivery of a teddy bear, I really started to feel uneasy. The teddy bear joined the flowers in the bin, and I gathered up the bag to take it out to the dumpster.

The next day, I waited in anticipation, hoping that there wouldn't be any more surprise gifts. Thankfully, the day was quiet. The next day, however, I heard another knock. The delivery kid handed me a plain brown box and walked away whistling while I just looked at the package in my hands, not knowing what to expect this time.

I set the box on my table and stared at it for a moment, half expecting to hear it ticking or something. Finally, I got a knife from the kitchen and carefully opened it. Inside was a mound of packing peanuts covering a box of chocolates. I noticed that the box was already open, missing the plastic wrapper that should have been there, which set off alarm bells in my mind. There was a note.

Since you didn't like my flowers or my bear, maybe my chocolates will be more to your liking. It's rude to throw out gifts, you know. But I'll let it slide this time. Enjoy the tasty treat, and I better not see this in your dumpster tomorrow. I'll be watching!

Stunned, I dropped the knife onto the table with a shaky hand. Who were these from? He was watching me? What the hell do I do? Did I go to the police? The note wasn't exactly threatening, not specifically. But the idea of someone watching me and checking my trash was sending chills down my spine. The walls of my flat, which had felt so homey, now seemed to be closing in on me. I opened the box of chocolates to see that they had all been bitten in half, each piece broken and out of place with obvious teeth marks. I put the lid back on the box, pushed it back into the packing peanuts, and took the whole thing to the bin. I wasn't going to put it in the dumpster, but I definitely wasn't going to eat them.

I was grateful that there was no knock on my door for a few days, but my paranoia didn't let up. Every time I walked to work, I felt eyes following me. When I would take my lunch breaks, I was so stressed and anxious that I barely had an appetite and would end up throwing most of my lunch in the bin.

After two weeks of no mystery gifts, though, I started to feel myself relax. Maybe he'd forgotten all about me. After sleeping in on a quiet Saturday morning, I decided to get out of the house and treat myself to the first nice meal I'd had in a long time. I took a cab to Little Italy, a cozy restaurant with the best pasta! I would normally have walked since it was only a 15-minute stroll from my flat, but it was still very chilly, and the drizzling rain hadn't let up in over 24 hrs.

The hostess sat me at a corner table near the window, and I browsed the menu, trying to decide between the spaghetti seafood or the lasagna al forno. Regardless of the entree, I had very quickly decided that I would follow it up with the chocolate orange ice cream that had just been added to the menu!

Just as I told the waitress that I had chosen the seafood option, I heard the front door open and in walked Cara, followed by Liam! I felt myself immediately blushing and tried to think of a casual way to hide under my table with the menu over my head. Before I had come up with a strategy to disappear, Cara spotted me and waved. Seeing that the rest of my table was empty, she pointed to me, and the waitress led them to my table.

Oh fuck, what am I going to say?

"Well, well, I didn't think I'd see you out and about today, Sarah." Cara grinned. "Mind if we join you?"

She sat down before I could utter a sound.

Liam at least had the decency to look somewhat embarrassed. He raised his eyebrow at me as if making sure I was ok with this arrangement before he took a seat. I gave him a small nod, and he pulled out the chair across the table from me.

"I haven't really seen much of you since that night at the

pub." Cara continued. "You left in such a hurry!"

"Cara," Liam growled low in a warning.

She quickly flipped him the bird and kept looking at me. "You really should have stuck around. Everyone was asking if you were going to sing another song! Even the DJ was asking where you went!"

I didn't know what to say. I never speak up for myself, never defend myself. I felt bad about calling Liam an asshole, but I was also starting to get pissed about Cara's pushiness.

"Well, I guess I left because I don't like being insulted," I said quietly.

Liam's face paled.

Cara laughed. "You mean what Liam said? Oh gods, girl, that was nothing! Besides, I'd told him all about your stories, the wild life you lead. He knows all about it."

It was my turn for the blood to drain from my face. Why would she have told him all those stories? Didn't she know those were almost 20 years ago? Did she really think I was still that person?

Liam gave me a pained, apologetic look.

Cara's phone rang and she had to dig through her huge purse before she found it. "Oh, it's Aislin. She's having issues with her new man. I'd better take this." She quickly left and walked out to the patio under the awning to stay out of the rain.

I didn't know what to say. I think I forgot how to speak at all. Liam cleared his throat nervously.

"I... I'm truly sorry. I shouldn't have listened to my sister. And I... I shouldn't have said the things I did. I know I upset you, and I'm sure you don't want to speak to me ever again, but I hope that you can find a bit of forgiveness for me."

I just stared at him for a moment. He seemed so genuinely sorry that I felt myself melting just a bit. I had to think of something to say and still try to keep my cool.

"I can probably do that," I said, giving him a shy smile. "I'm pretty sure I said a few things I shouldn't have as well."

Liam's expression warmed. "Oh, like calling me an asshole?"

My grin widened a smidge. "Well, I'm still not sure I was wrong about that, but I probably shouldn't have called you out on it."

I was rewarded with a hearty laugh. "Ah, Princess. It seems you already know me so well!"

I didn't want to tell him that it was he who seemed to know me, the way he was revealing my innermost thoughts and secrets. I decided to change the subject.

"Princess? Still going with that, huh?"

He shrugged. "It's not an inaccurate nickname. I figured as long as I don't add anything else to it, I would be safe."

Before I could respond, Cara returned to the table, obviously upset.

"I'm so sorry, Li. Aislin needs me. She got into a huge fight with Tony, and she's on the verge of throwing all his shite into the street. I've got to go over there and calm her down."

"It's fine, Cara, we can go."

She shook her head and gave him a quick wink. "Naw, you can stay here, enjoy your meal! I'm sure you two have loads to talk about! I'll see you later, bye!"

And with that, she was out the door, hailing a cab. Liam gave me a sheepish look.

"Would you mind if I stayed? I can leave too if you're uncomfortable."

Would I mind? Having a meal with the finest man I'd seen in years? Just because he has a way of reading my mind and making me forget how to form sentences... Why would I mind?

I tried to appear indifferent, but I'm afraid I wasn't able to successfully pull it off. "I mean, you're already here; you may as well order. It's fine with me."

He smiled, as if he could see that I was flustered, but didn't comment on it. Instead, he flagged down the waitress to place his order. Without looking at the menu, he ordered the exact same meal as I had, and I wasn't sure if that was a coincidence or not.

While we waited for our food, the conversation was light and easy. What did I think of Inverness so far? What kind of movies and music did we like? Had I seen the latest episode of Doctor Who? That led into a detailed discussion on who was the best Doctor and why. We were still debating Daleks versus Cybermen when the waitress brought our food to the table.

I was surprised at how much we had in common and how easily we could talk about all kinds of things. It was still very much a surface-level conversation, but it felt comfortable until he asked me why I would take a job overseas and leave my life in the States behind.

Not knowing if I should give the quick answer or the honest one, I decided to be honest.

"I, uh... I didn't really have much to leave behind. I don't have much family, not that I speak to anyone anyway. I have one cousin whom I adore, and she was actually the one who encouraged me to take this job opportunity. She said it was Karma paying me back for all the shit I've been through in my life."

He gave me a questioning gaze. "Gone through it, have ya?"

I nodded. "Yeah, it's been rough over the years. I lost my mom several years ago, and that almost broke me. A bad marriage that... well, let's just say I was lucky to get out of. It did cause some permanent issues, not being able to have kids, for instance."

I had tried to say that as casually as I could, not wanting to make a big deal out of it, but I could see Liam's fist clenching his napkin so tightly that his knuckles were white.

"How... what happened to cause that?"

Not knowing how I should answer his question, I just looked down at my lap.

"I'm sorry," he whispered. "I shouldn't have asked that; it's too personal."

"It's ok. I just don't usually bring it up in a first conversation because it's kind of heavy and most people don't like to talk about stuff like that."

He reached across the table and nudged my hand to get me to

look up at him. "I'm not most people."

The first sting of tears hit my eyes, and I blinked them away. "I can see that. Well... I mean, if you really want to know..."

"I do."

I nodded. "I was stupid and didn't see the hilltop of red flags. I had just been dumped when I met Ben, and he made me feel special, important. I fell hard and fast for him. And you know, things were good at first. But the fights evolved into pushes, pushes into slaps, slaps into... more."

I was proud of myself for not letting my voice tremble as I told my story. When I dared meet his gaze, I saw a volcanic eruption in those dark green eyes. He didn't interrupt me, just nodded for me to continue.

"I didn't know what love bombing was. So when he would buy me flowers afterward, I thought he really was sorry, so I forgave him. But the longer I stayed, the worse it got. Eventually, it went beyond physical abuse. He got creative in his... torture. At one point, he told me I would be a bad wife if I didn't let him... share me."

Liam's voice was low and rumbled across the table. "Share you?"

I couldn't look at him. "Yes. With his friends."

"Mac a' ghalla!" he muttered.

I frowned at the phrase, and he shook his head. "Sorry, keep going, if you want to."

"Well, like I said, he evolved, starting to do new things to keep himself interested. Used objects that weren't meant to be used in that way. One day, he went too far and... broke something. I spent several days in the hospital, and by the time they released me, the chance of having kids was less than five percent. It's odd because I knew I didn't want kids with him. I'd never put them through anything like that. But it was that moment that made me decide to leave him. I had gotten used to the pain and the abuse, convinced that it was as good as I was ever going to get. But when he took that from me, that dream of being a mother, I'd had enough. I packed my bags and left."

I watch Liam draw a shaky breath. It looked as though he was having trouble finding words. I immediately felt guilty for dumping my past on him and began to apologize.

"I shouldn't have said all that. You didn't want to know about all that shit. I'm so sorry."

He held up a hand to stop me. Taking in another deep breath, he looked directly into my eyes. "Never be sorry for telling your story. It's part of what makes you YOU." He gently took hold of my hand. "I'm the one who's sorry. Sorry you ever went through anything like that. You... you didn't deserve that."

I felt my face grow hot under his stare. "Uh, I... th... thank you, Liam." I could tell that there was more that he wanted to say, but he kept it to himself. The weight of my story seemed to hang in the air between us, not as a burden but as something powerful that had created a connection. How or why, I wasn't sure, but something about that feeling made the barrier around my heart crack slightly.

The waitress took that moment to bring us our checks. Before I could say a word, Liam grabbed both tickets and handed the server his card. I started to protest, but he held up his hand again. It was like a magic spell the way he could stop me with such a simple gesture.

"I've got it, no worries, Princess. It's my honor."

I didn't know what to say, so I kept silent. When he signed the receipt, we stood to leave, and Liam helped me with my coat. He flagged down a taxi and offered it to me.

"I'll get the next one."

Opening the door for me, he put a hand on my shoulder. "I enjoyed this. I know that you think things got to be too much, too heavy. But I promise, I don't mind. Talks like that help people learn about each other. And I'm glad I learned more about you. I'm just sorry you had to deal with all that."

"Thanks, Liam. I really appreciate that." Without thinking, I leaned in to give him a one-armed hug. Mid-move, I panicked. What am I doing? It had just felt like the natural thing to do in the moment. I was about to pull back when his arm pulled me in and finished the hug. He felt so solid and warm in the chilly air. I wanted to stay right there.

As he pulled back, he smiled. "Maybe we could do this again sometime?"

I returned his smile. "I... I'd like that."

He took my elbow and helped me into the taxi. Talk about old school gentleman... who was this guy? The cab pulled away, and I couldn't help the goofy grin on my face. But it disappeared when I had a sudden, horrible thought.

"I didn't get his number!"

The entire following week, I argued with myself about whether or not I should just ask Cara for her brother's number. It seemed like such a simple thing to ask for, but I knew it would lead to questions and probably teasing, and I didn't think I was ready to face any of that. So I just replayed that lunch over and over in my mind.

The self-doubt of his final words wound their way into my mind. Surely he was just being nice. No one who sat through a conversation like that would want to spend time with me again. I'm too much for people, too many traumas and issues to deal with. How many times had people told me that when I finally brought up the subject of my past?

That Friday, when I opened the door to leave for work, I was shocked to see there was another package from my stalker lying on my doorstep, waiting for me. I was already running late, so I just picked it up and continued on my way to the office. I set the package on my desk, planning on ignoring it until my lunch break, when I would be able to throw away whatever was in there at work, where hopefully he wouldn't know. But when I left my first meeting, Cara and Aislin were at my cubicle laughing.

"Oooh, someone's got great taste!" Cara giggled.

"Aye, I didn't think you had it in you, Sarah!" Aislin joined in.

"Well, not in her yet!" Cara replied, sending Aislin into another fit of laughter.

I looked at what Aislin was holding in her hands and felt the color drain from my face. It was a dog collar, leash, and a bright purple ball gag. Cara was also holding a small item which she waved in my direction.

"A vibrating butt plug? Really, Sarah, at the office?"

I didn't know what to say. I was humiliated and terrified. Memories of my past traumas flashed through my mind. I grabbed my purse and ran to my boss's office to make some excuse of not feeling well, and quickly went home. Every person I passed on my way back to my flat made me jump; every glance my way felt threatening. When I got to my doorstep, I saw yet another box. Written on the top in bold letters was a short message.

"DO NOT IGNORE ME."

I gingerly picked up the box and quickly opened my door to rush inside. Turning the lock behind me, I opened the box in fear. Inside was a leather whip and another note. "I'll forgive you for cheating on me at the Italian place. I know you're mine. And I know that you like it rough and dirty. I'll find out for myself soon enough. I wouldn't tell anyone about this, though. It's going to be our little secret. See you soon, my dirty whore!"

The tears burned my eyes as I threw the note to the floor. What was I going to do? I had no one to talk to; I barely knew anyone here. I had a brief thought that I wish I could call Liam, but that vanished quickly, knowing I couldn't be a burden to him. I went into my bedroom, crawled into bed, and sobbed.

LIAM

S.E. WALKER

Hoisting the engine up with the cherry picker, Liam started to gather his tools and got ready to work. His best friend had brought this motorcycle to him for a thorough overhaul, and he should have had this done days ago. Rebuilding and working on engines not only seemed to come naturally to him, but it usually helped clear his mind. Lately, though, nothing could shake the image of Sarah, first up on that stage, then the fire in her eyes when she clapped back at his stupid comments, and finally watching her tell him the story of her past. Replaying that moment in his mind over and over, his anger grew, and he found himself wanting to wrap her in his arms and take all her pain away. But he had been so stupid and forgot to get her number. His frustration grew, and he let out a yell, throwing his wrench across the garage.

"Is the engine giving you that much trouble?"

Startled, he turned around to see his mate Declan. He hadn't even heard the truck pull up; he was so distracted. Seeing his friend immediately made him feel a bit better. Since primary school, they had been thick as thieves, despite their drastic differences. While Liam looked more like a Viking at his height of 6'2", Declan was broad but about six inches shorter. His shoulder-length black hair was always pulled back with a leather tie, and he had blue eyes that were always sparkling with laughter. Over their teenage years, the two boys had found themselves involved in fights, minor vandalism, petty theft, and other typical troubles. Their mothers had spent many a Sunday begging their priest for help with the unruly boys.

As they grew up, there were still occasional bar fights, but they had matured past any criminal activity. Declan had been the one to help pull Liam out of his depression, and Fiona and Liam knew that he was alive today because of this man.

Sighing, he laughed. "I hate to tell ye this, brother, but I haven't even started."

Declan pretended to be shocked. "What are you talkin' about, mate? The great Liam MacKay is slacking when he should be putting all his time and effort into fixing my old bike. I can't believe it!"

Liam shook his head and threw an oil rag at Declan's head. "I swear I'm getting to it."

Declan caught the rag and threw it back. "I know, mate. I just wanted to come around to check in on ya. Colin called me and said you could use a visit. I thought the two of us could take a couple of your bikes up to the hills and see the sights."

It was something they had done since they were young, anytime either of them needed to get away, clear their mind, or talk. Grateful, Liam nodded and tossed Declan the keys to one of the bikes, grabbing two helmets from hooks on the wall. Declan pulled a small cooler from the back of his truck, putting it into his bike's saddle bag, and without a word, they fired up the engines and roared their way up into the mountains.

After a while, they stopped at a hilltop pull-off, shut down the bikes, and found a place to sit along the railing overlooking the valley below. Declan pulled out the cooler and tossed Liam a lager. Neither said anything for several minutes, just enjoying the view. After a while, Declan broke the silence.

"So tell me about her."

Knowing there was no point in pretending he didn't know who Declan was referring to, he just took a drag of his lager. "Her name is Sarah. She's a Yank who works with Cara. I thought it was going to be another one of Cara's stupid setups, but mate... when I got to the pub, she was on the stage singing. I've never heard anything so beautiful. And she was... she looked killer! These eyes that could see right through my soul."

"She sounds great, mate."

Liam nodded, "More than that. She was perfect. Then I had to go and fuck it up by listening to my shite sister about how Sarah was some sort of freak and wanted a guy who would be all dark and dominating. I opened my fucking mouth and said something dumb about her being a bad girl and a dirty princess."

Declan burst out laughing. "What the hell, mate? A dirty princess? Why princess?"

Liam just lowered his head with a rueful laugh. "It's what

'Sarah' means. And I know. I was a fucking eejit."

"Agreed! What did she say to that?"

"She snapped back with a comment about my name meaning 'ignorant' or 'fucking asshole' and then left."

Declan took another swing and shrugged. "She sounds like a helluva woman."

Sighing, Liam nodded. "She is. I mean, I don't really know her yet, technically. But we ran into each other last weekend. Ended up having lunch and talking. Fucking hell, Dec. The things she's been through would tear anyone apart, but her? She's so strong and she doesn't even know it!"

"What kind of things?"

Liam groaned as if the thought of it caused him physical pain. "Her ex... the fucker beat the shite out of her regularly. Then let his friends... he shared her with them, Declan!"

"Jesus Christ!"

"I just want to tear his head off with my bare hands!" Liam growled.

"I understand, brother. I feel the same way. Anyone who could do something so vile deserves more than that. But tell me something. Do you feel this way because it's just a natural thing after hearing a story like that, or... is it because of Sarah, specifically?"

Liam stilled. "What do you mean?"

Giving his friend a long look, Declan shook his head. "Liam, we've been mates since we were wee lads, and through all the women I've seen you with, even Fiona, I've never seen you this undone. If one night at a pub for ten minutes and one short but intense conversation with her has done this to you, it means something. I wouldn't ignore it. If I were you, I'd see where this could go. I know your first meeting with her made her think you're an asshole, which, let's face it, you may be on occasion, but only when it's called for." He got serious and clapped Liam on the shoulder. "You're a good man, Liam. You deserve to be happy."

Feeling his heart swell with affection for his friend, Liam

nodded. He couldn't think of the words to say in response, but he also knew that words weren't needed. They took in the view for a few more minutes, finishing their lagers, then climbed back onto their bikes and rode back to Liam's shop.

Liam hadn't been home for five minutes when his phone rang. Family dinners didn't happen often, but when his ma called to say that she wanted her children gathered at her house, he knew better than to argue. He walked through the kitchen door at his ma's house to see Cara and the middle brother Colin already sitting at the table. His ma walked over and stood on her tiptoes to kiss his cheek.

"Welcome home, love."

He hadn't lived at home in over twenty years, but she always said that when he came over. He smiled and kissed the top of her head.

"Halo, Ma. Ciamar a tha thu?" He clapped Colin on the shoulder and gave Cara a quick peck on the cheek. "How'd you two beat me here?"

Cara just smiled, "You're always the last to arrive, Li."

He couldn't argue the point, as he noticed the food was already done and his mother was bringing the dishes to the table. They fell into familiar banter and conversation, teasing jokes and catching up on the latest news. When Cara started a story about something funny at work, Liam's ears pricked up.

"Aislin and I couldn't help but open the box. We saw the logo on the side, and we knew which shop it was. And would you believe it? It was a butt plug! Ball gag and all! I thought Sarah was going to die right there. It was hilarious!"

"Cara Marie MacKay, I'll have none of that talk at my table!" their mother protested, but she was mostly ignored.

"Someone sent her a box with that shite in it?" Liam questioned.

Cara nodded. "It just had her name on it, no address. But it said 'from your secret friend' on the top, so I don't know who it was from. You should have seen her face!"

Liam's mind was spinning. He hadn't been able to stop

thinking about Sarah since their lunch date, no matter how hard he had tried, and after his conversation with Declan, he had already decided that he was going to try and find a way to see her again. Hearing that someone was sending her sex toys made his blood boil for a reason he couldn't pin down. Was it that he was jealous? Or angry? He couldn't tell, but he was definitely not pleased to hear this story.

"Did... did she seem happy about the gift?" He asked awkwardly.

Cara frowned. "No, not really. Actually, she left it there and ran out. She hasn't been back to the office since last Friday, so it's been over a week. Yesterday she said she was sick and worked from home. I put the box in the boot of my car to get it out of the office. I figured I'd give it to her the next time she came in, but it didn't seem like she wanted it."

Liam jumped up, grabbed Cara's coat to get her keys, and ran out to her car. Opening the boot, he saw the box and the block lettering on the top. He opened it, his teeth grinding when he saw the toys inside. He dumped them out and saw the note that fluttered down from the bottom of the box. Feeling only slightly guilty for snooping, he opened the folded paper.

"Just a little preview of what's to come. I know you're a dirty little whore, and I'm going to show you who owns you. Don't forget to keep our little secret! See you soon!"

Remembering that Cara said Sarah did not look happy about this gift, his blood began to boil. Was she in trouble? He took the note and slammed the boot closed, seeing Cara standing next to the car, staring at him.

"What are ye doin', Li?"

"Did you see this when you were going through the box?" He held the note out to her.

She read it silently, suddenly serious. "Naw, I didn't. Li, I don't like the sound of this. I didn't realize it at the time, but she looked scared. What... what does it mean?"

"It means that I think she's got some sick stalker, Cara. And ye were just laughing at her!" He growled.

"I... I didn't know! I thought it was just a joke from someone she knew." Cara stammered.

"Do ye have her number? Have you called to check on her?"

Cara shook her head. "I have her number, but I didn't think to call her. I thought she was just not feeling well."

"Where is her flat? Do you know?"

"I don't know which flat is hers, but I think she lives in Frisco Villas on Fairfield Rd."

Liam nodded and got into his car. He didn't know what he was doing exactly. Something in his gut was telling him Sarah was in danger, and the thought was twisting him up. He didn't know her; he didn't know why he hadn't been able to stop thinking about her, but the idea that someone was stalking or threatening her turned his mind dark. His tires spun as he pulled away from the house and raced down the road. The sun was already setting and the light fading into the night as he made his way across town toward Fairfield Rd.

SARAH

I had been putting off taking my trash out for two weeks, but my bins were full of rotting food scraps and boxes from the crazy stalker, and I needed to take them to the dumpster. Finding some inner determination, I put my coat on over my pjs, slipped on my shoes, and put a kitchen knife in my coat pocket. I picked up the bins and walked out into the night. Just as I finished emptying the second bin, I heard a sound behind me. I dropped the bins and put my hand into my pocket for the knife and turned quickly. In the shadow of the alley was a figure slowly moving toward me. I squinted my eyes to try and make out any features as he got closer.

"I told ya I'd be seeing you soon." His voice sent chills through me. As he moved into the light from the street, I finally saw his face, straining my memory to recognize him. It took me a moment, but finally it clicked. From the pub... he was the DJ! He knew my name from the sign-up sheet that night. That must have been how he found me! OMG, what was I going to do? I pulled the knife out of my pocket, and he just laughed.

"Ya think a little knife like that is going to do anything? You should know that's not going to stop me. You're mine! I've been sending you so many gifts. Don't you know how I feel? I heard you sing that night and I could feel it. When you looked at me after your song, I knew you were singing for me."

He kept moving closer, and I tried to step back, but I was up against the dumpster with nowhere to go.

"I wasn't singing for you, you asshole. It was just a song, I didn't even pick it out myself!"

He gave a wicked laugh. "Oi, don't play dumb now. I saw how you were dressed that night, too. You were trying to get attention. And you got mine, didn't ya?"

I shook my head. "I wasn't! I don't even know you!" Tears were spilling down my cheeks.

"You do know me. All the things I've sent to ya, you know who I am. And I know who you are. You're my little whore, aren't ya?"

Trembling, I tried to catch my breath. "NO!" I turned to try and run, but he was close enough to grab my wrist and shake it hard enough that I dropped the knife. He spun me around to face him and pushed me against the dumpster. He leaned in and drew a deep breath against my neck.

"Ah, I can smell ya, dirty girl. You're all mine!"

I've never been in a fight in my life, but at that moment, my fight-or-flight instinct kicked in, and I tried to kick him in the balls and pull my wrist free from his grip, but he was too strong.

"Ah ah ah, none of those games. Don't play coy, slut. Don't pretend you don't want me."

"I don't!" I sobbed.

He pinned my arms behind me and held me in place. "Don't lie to me!" Suddenly, his fist hit my gut, and my breath was gone. Pain shot through me, and I doubled over. He pulled me upright again and backhanded me, splitting my lip. I could taste blood, and my face felt like it was on fire.

"Aye, you like it rough, don't ya?"

I tried to shake my head, but his fist found me again, this time to my left temple. I saw stars and my knees gave out beneath me.

"Ah, that's a good little whore, lay down for me."

I felt his weight on top of me, felt him slide his hand up my tank top, squeezing my breast so hard I gasped. I tried to scream, but my lungs wouldn't cooperate, so I just wiggled around enough to pull myself out from under him and try to roll away. He growled in frustration and quickly stood so he could kick me in the ribs. I had never felt a pain like that, and I curled up as tight as I could to protect myself. He kicked again and reached down to grab me by the hair and pull my head up.

"Stop fighting me. You'll like it, just relax."

With my body halfway upright, hanging from his grip, I found enough air to let out a loud scream.

"Shut up, ye slut!" He slapped me again, my head hitting the ground this time so hard that I almost blacked out. Trying to focus my eyes, I could feel him pulling my pajama shorts so they tore away. His fingertips brushed against the most sensitive skin. I screamed again, and he just laughed and tore my underwear off, ripping the fabric to shreds.

My mind was suddenly back in that space of submission that my ex forced me to develop. A way to survive and take myself out of the situation I was in, to mentally escape and not feel what was happening. I stopped moving, stopping screaming. I just was. Shrinking into myself, waiting for it to be over.

I focused on the feel of the concrete below me, the pebbles and litter pushing into my skin. I smelled the rank rotten food and garbage in the bin behind my head. The way the cold air was such a contrast to the heat of the man's body on mine. It was all objective thoughts, like I wasn't really the one being attacked; I was just an observer.

Just as he started to undo the zipper on his jeans, I heard a shout from the street.

"Sarah?!"

I felt the man above me freeze, heard him curse under his breath, then lean down and whisper in my ear.

"Guess it's not the night for us tonight, my little whore. You'll just have to wait for me. I'll be back! Don't you dare call the police, or next time you won't survive my visit! And if you tell anyone about this, I'll hunt them all down, and before I kill them, I'll make them watch as I take you."

With that, he gave me one more hard kick to the ribs and ran off into the dark. I could hear the voice still calling for me.

"Sarah?! Where are ye?"

I tried to sit up, but the pain was excruciating. I gathered all the strength I could muster and let out a weak, "I'm here!"

I saw a man run into the alley between the building where I was and the ground. When he saw me, he stopped short in a brief moment of shock, then ran to me.

"Oh gods, Sarah!" I heard him say quietly. He knelt down, assessing me. When I was able to raise my eyes, difficult because I was still dizzy from the blow to my head, I looked up into Liam's horrified face.

"Liam?" I whispered.

"I've got to get you to hospital!" Looking down at my bruised body, he noticed my torn panties next to me, and I swear he looked as though he were about to cry.

"No!" I croaked. "No hospitals!" The thought of painkillers from the hospital sounded wonderful, but I knew that a trip to the emergency department would also mean a call to the police, and I couldn't risk that.

"Are ye serious? You need to see a doctor!"

I grabbed his arm, pleading. "No hospital! Promise me!" My desperation seemed to pull at something, and his expression changed.

"Ok, I promise."

Relieved, I let go of his arm. The pain in my ribs and stomach, plus the pounding in my head, suddenly overwhelmed me, and my vision went black as I fainted.

LIAM

He pulled up to the first building in the Frisco Villas area, parking his car along the curb. He wasn't sure what his plan was, going door to door maybe? Someone would surely know who Sarah was and which flat was hers. He ran up one row and knocked on the first door, but no lights were on and it seemed like no one was home. Before he could reach the second door, he heard a scream from a few rows down. That scream sent ice through his veins.

"Sarah?!" He called out, trying to figure out which direction the sound had come from. Running back onto the street, he saw a figure running out of an alley, but there wasn't enough light for him to make out any details. He started to follow, but as he reached the opening of the alley, he looked to his right to see Sarah lying on the ground near the bins. All thoughts of chasing down the figure vanished, and he ran to her side. Her face was bloody and bruised, a lump starting to form on her temple, her lip cut, and she was holding her stomach, curled up into a little ball on the concrete. Fighting back a surge of rage, he noticed that she was naked from the waist down, her underwear in tatters beside her. He knelt down shakily.

"Oh gods, Sarah!" The way she looked up at him with unfocused eyes broke his heart. All he could think was he needed to get her help as quickly as possible.

"NO! No hospitals!"

He couldn't understand why she was refusing to see a doctor, but the sheer desperation in her gaze stopped his protests.

"Ok, I promise."

She passed out then, and his heart lurched in his chest. Not knowing what else to do, he pulled her into his arms as gently as he could. Looking around, he didn't know which door was hers, and it didn't feel safe to take her to her own flat anyway, so he carried her to his car. He laid her in the back seat, putting his coat over her, then jumped into the driver's seat. His house was 30 km away, but he didn't have any other choice. He was picking up his phone as he started the engine. After two rings, his brother Colin answered.

"What's up, Li?" Colin sounded concerned, likely worried by the way Liam had rushed out in the middle of dinner.

"Colin, I need you to meet me at my place NOW!"

"What happened, Liam?"

"I don't have time. I just need your help. I'll meet you there!" Liam hung up without waiting for a reply and sped down the road towards home. As he drove, his anger fueled unwanted memories to flood his brain.

He was only ten years old when he heard his mother shouting from the upstairs bedroom. His dad had been on another one of his benders, out all weekend with the lads. It wasn't unusual for him to come home in a drunken rage and take it out on his wife, but most of the time, it was just a few slaps or a rare punch, and Maggie kept quiet because she never wanted the children to know. Liam and Colin always knew, however, and they would sneak into baby Cara's room to keep her quiet, fearing that Thomas's anger might turn towards them. Then, when Thomas would pass out, the boys would help their mother get cleaned up, dress any wounds she might have, and hold her hands while she cried quietly.

But that night, as Liam heard his mother cry out, he knew that this time was different. He tiptoed to their bedroom door and peeked in. Thomas was shoving Maggie onto the bed and had ripped her dress down the front. She already had a black eye and a massive bruise on her neck from his hand squeezing her throat.

"Ye think ye can talk back to me, woman? I'll show you your place. You belong to me!"

As he watched his father slap his mother again, push her onto the bed, and kneel down on the floor between her legs, something inside Liam's young mind snapped. He knew that if he didn't do something, this evil man was going to kill his mother. Without a second guess, he went downstairs and found the butcher knife in the kitchen. Silently, he went back to the bedroom and sneaked up behind his father. His mother had barely had a chance to meet Liam's eyes when he struck, jamming the knife into his father's throat.

Thomas gurgled as the blood began to pour over Maggie's legs and the bed covers. Maggie gasped in horror and quickly grabbed her son to pull him away. They held each other in silence and watched as Thomas struggled to speak. His eyes sparked with anger, shock, and betrayal, but it didn't take long for him to bleed out, falling to the floor without a sound.

Maggie dropped to her knees, made the sign of the cross, and wept. Liam stood deathly still, staring at his father on the floor. He wasn't scared; he knew that it was the right thing to do, to protect his Ma. He had no regrets, but he wasn't sure what would happen next.

They stayed there for a moment, neither saying a word, just staring at the body of the man who had caused them all so much pain. Liam noticed that now his father didn't look so large and imposing. He actually looked fragile. Glancing down at his mother, he saw her staring past Thomas, as if she were seeing something beyond him, her free hand clutching the torn dress shut against her chest. Silent tears were drying on her face, and Liam could smell her perfume mixed with the clean smell of the laundry soap and the bread that she had baked for dinner that night. The smells that always seemed familiar are now etched into his mind as the smell of his mother in that moment. The strong woman who endured so much but never let her children suffer the same as she did. The woman who hid her bruises while making sure her children were fed and safe.

He felt his ma take hold of his hand and whisper, "Go clean yerself and go to your room. I have to phone the police." She looked up at him. "When they ask ye what happened, you tell them you don't know. You saw nothing. It was I who did this; it was self-defense. They all know what kind of man Thomas was; they'll be thanking me for ridding the world of him. But you had nothing to do with it, understood?"

Liam nodded and went to the loo to wash the splatters of blood off his hands. He threw his pajamas into the basket and walked stiffly back to his room. Colin was still in Cara's room, so Liam quickly put clean pajamas on and crawled into bed, listening to the sound of his mother's voice on the telephone. Soon, two policemen knocked on the door and Maggie led them upstairs.

"Ah fookin' hell, Maggie!" one of them cried.

"Did he do that to yer face?" The other asked.

Maggie quietly told them about the beating and how she had put the knife by the bed, knowing that Thomas would be coming home drunk and in one of his moods. She said he was choking her when she reached for it. She didn't really know what she was doing, but she knew he was going to kill her. The policemen muttered their understanding, knowing all too well what Thomas MacKay was like. The rest of the night was a blur of police and finally the coroner coming to take the body away. While the children were asked if they saw anything, no one questioned Maggie's story, and no charges were brought against her. The whole village knew Thomas, and no one was surprised that his life ended this way or that Maggie had finally had enough of his fists.

Jerking himself free of that memory, Liam brought his focus back to the road. No one had ever learned the truth about that night, except for Colin, who Liam had confided in many years later. Fearing judgment, Liam was relieved to hear Colin approve.

"I remember that night, her screams. Honestly, Li, if you hadn't done it, I would have."

Knowing that his brother always had his back, he knew Colin was the one who would help him now. He had to make sure that Sarah was not only ok physically, but safe emotionally. Knowing what abuse like that could do to any woman, and knowing she had been through this hell already in her life, he felt a determination well up in him to find this sick fuck and make sure he never hurt Sarah or anyone else ever again.

SARAH

I felt a pillow under my head and a soft blanket tucked around my shoulders. There was a warm washcloth over my eyes blocking my vision. I tried to move, but even the smallest change in my position caused pain to shoot through my body. I must have groaned because I was suddenly aware of a hand on my forearm. Terrified of someone I couldn't see touching me, I tried to scream and pull away.

"Sarah, Princess, it's ok! It's me, Liam!"

I stopped at his voice and reached up to pull the cloth off my eyes. I could barely see out of them, but I could make out his blurry face looking at me with concern. I felt myself relax, but everything that had happened flooded my mind, and the tears started to pour. The pressure in my head from crying only made the tears flow faster.

"Oh fuck..." I felt his hand on the side of my face, gently wiping away my tears. I turned into his hand and tried to stop crying.

"She's awake?" I hear another voice call from across the room. I stiffened.

"It's ok, Princess. It's my brother Colin. He's an EMT. I promised I wouldn't take you to the hospital, but I didn't say I wouldn't find a way to help you. You need medical attention."

I knew he was right. Every breath caused pain to spike through my chest, and my stomach felt like, well, like someone had kicked me several times. My head was pounding and my wrist throbbed from being twisted around behind my back, my fingers were tingling, and I was having trouble wiggling them.

Colin knelt down to my level to assess me now that I was awake. I tried to look around, and I saw that I was lying on a couch in a cozy living room. A warm fire was crackling in the corner. While the room looked nice and homey, I didn't recognize anything. Where was I?

As if reading my mind, Liam spoke softly, "I brought you to my place. I... I didn't know which flat was yours, and I thought it was probably better to get you away from where... well... from that place."

I nodded sadly. I didn't want to be anywhere near that building. Colin was feeling my wrist, gingerly probing the joints.

"It's not broken, but it's sprained for sure." He reached over to his bag to pull out a bandage to wrap around it. "I know it's going to hurt, but I need to feel for broken ribs and any other injuries. Is that ok?"

I didn't really want to be touched, but I knew he was only trying to help, and I really did need to be checked out. I nodded again, and he helped me slowly sit up. The pain almost made me black out again. As I fought the feeling, I focused on what else I could feel and sense around me besides my pain. I suddenly realized that I didn't have my pajama shorts on, remembering that everything had been ripped off. I blushed deeply and pulled the blanket tightly over my lap and held it to my chest. My coat was gone, and all I was wearing was my torn tank top, one thin strap hanging down.

"Uh, I... I can give you some privacy." Liam stuttered. "But here, I found your glasses next to you and I picked them up for you." He handed me my frames, and I took them gratefully.

"Don't put them on yet. I need to check to make sure you don't have a concussion." Colin said.

I just held my glasses in my lap and sat still, trying to find a way to inhale without crying. Liam walked away slowly, obviously not wanting to leave but wanting to save me from the embarrassment of barely being dressed. I really appreciated that.

Colin tried to be as gentle as he could as he felt my ribs and stomach, looking for injuries. I whimpered when he pried my eyelids open to check my pupils with a bright light. He was thorough and professional, but I could sense that he was holding back anger at what I had been through. Finally, he sat back on his heels and looked at me.

"Without an X-ray, I can't say for sure, but I've patched up enough bar fights to say you've definitely got a cracked rib or two, though I don't feel any that are broken fully. I can wrap you up to help keep them still and make it a touch easier to breathe.

Your wrist is sprained, you've got some major bruising, possibly some internal injuries, but again, without a scan, I can't say how bad they are. Your vision seems clear, so I don't think you're concussed, but you'll probably have a helluva headache for a while. Let's get you standing so I can wrap up those ribs. Then I'm going to wash and disinfect your legs."

I looked down, surprised. The pain in my torso and head had been so bad, I hadn't even realized that my legs had several cuts and scrapes, likely from falling onto the littered concrete of the alleyway and crawling away from... I shook my head to try and stop myself from reliving the moment. I tried to take his hand and stand on my feet, but my legs didn't want to hold me. Liam was suddenly there, his hands under my arms pulling me up. He held me there with ease while Colin pulled at my tank top.

"I know it's awkward, but I need to get this on without your shirt. Is that alright?"

I winced, but knew he was right, and he was a medical professional, so I shouldn't feel embarrassed. I took a quick glance back at Liam.

As if reading my thoughts, he gave me a small comforting smile. "I won't look," and he turned his head away.

I looked back at Colin and nodded. He raised my shirt up above my breasts and tapped Liam's fingers, indicating that he should help pull it up over my head. Once my shirt was gone, I was completely naked, and while I should have felt more exposed than I had earlier, I only felt a slight embarrassment. Mostly, I felt like I was finally safe.

Colin began winding the bandage around my ribs, and his expression darkened. I glanced down to see what he was looking at. A grotesque hand-shaped bruise was forming on my left breast. Colin shot a quick look at Liam, who, despite promising not to look, followed Colin's subtle nod to my bruised body. Rage burned in Liam's eyes, and he quickly turned away again as Colin continued to wrap my ribs. The bandage was tight, and it smashed my breasts down, which wasn't very comfortable, but I did feel less exposed.

Once Colin had finished, he took my arm to help steady me, and I felt Liam walk away. I turned as best I could to see him leaving the room, only to come back a second later with a t-shirt. It was too big, but it was soft and smelled like fresh laundry soap. The two men helped me pull the shirt down over the wrap around my rib cage and slowly lowered me back onto the couch. Liam pulled the blanket up and placed it around my shoulders, sitting next to me while Colin started getting the disinfectant ready for my cuts. When he began washing them out, I hissed in pain, and Liam grabbed my hand in support.

"Deep breath, Princess." He encouraged.

I rolled my eyes at him. "You try taking a deep breath with cracked ribs!" I growled.

He let out a laugh. "You think I haven't had a cracked rib or two in my life?" I could see the amusement in his eyes, mixed with concern for my pain. "I know how bad it feels. But if you hold your breath, it will only get worse. Breathe with me." He took in a slow breath, watching me to make sure I did the same. I fought through the pain and inhaled with him.

"And out through your mouth." He exhaled slowly and steadily. I followed suit. We repeated it three times, and I stopped noticing the sting on my legs while Colin cleaned the scrapes and taped bandages over them. Then he wiped the dried blood from my lower lip and cleaned the cut, finally dabbing a bit of cream on the split skin to keep it from drying out and cracking.

"Ok, that's about all I can do for you for now. Except I will give you something for pain." He reached into his bag and pulled out a bottle of pills. "These are strong; you're definitely going to sleep, but that's probably best. If you haven't eaten in a while, I would recommend something small before you take them. One at a time, every six hours as you need them. But the first 24 hours will be the worst. You should start to feel a wee bit better after that. Sleep as much as you can, ok?"

I nodded, "Thank you, Colin. I really appreciate your help and... and not asking questions."

He looked at me for a moment, then tilted his head in

acknowledgment. "Liam said you needed my help, and that's what brothers do. I don't need to know what happened, but I can guess. But that does lead me to a question I do have to ask. Uh, did...I mean, were you..." He flushed, "I should also make sure... er... were you sexually assaulted?"

I felt Liam go still beside me, waiting for my answer with dread.

I swallowed the lump in my throat and shivered. "Um... he ... he was going to. He was trying..." I began shaking at the memory, and I heard a crack as Liam's hand gripped the arm of the couch so hard that he broke the wood. Colin's eyes flashed with anger, but he stayed still and professional as I continued, "But he heard Liam's voice and ran off, so no. No, I wasn't."

Liam let out the breath he'd been holding with a soft sigh of relief. Colin gave a quick nod and stood.

"Ok, good. That's good. Well, if you need any help making a report, I know a couple of PC's I can call. Just let me know."

"Thanks, but it's not necessary," I said too quickly. He frowned but didn't question me.

He did give Liam a look I couldn't read, and the brothers gave each other a quick hug. Colin left and Liam sat back down at my side, staying on the very edge of the cushion as if to give me as much space as possible.

"Are ye hungry? Col said you needed to eat before you take one of those pills."

I started to shake my head. I just wanted to sleep and try to forget what happened, but as if on cue, my stomach growled loudly. I looked up at the clock hanging on the wall to see that it was almost midnight. I hadn't eaten anything since 4 pm and I was actually feeling a little hungry.

"I could eat something," I said shyly. He patted my hand and got up to rummage around in his kitchen.

"I have some leftover roast. I can make you a sandwich. Or I have a frozen pizza in here I could throw into the oven, if you want to wait a bit."

"A sandwich is fine, thank you," I called to him, trying to sit back as comfortably as possible with no luck.

"I've got ye," he replied. I could hear him pulling cabinet doors open, the rattle of the silverware drawer. A few minutes later, he brought over a TV tray and set it in front of me. There was a plate with the most delicious looking sandwich I'd ever seen, a handful of crisps, and a steaming mug of tea. The sandwich had a thick piece of tender looking beef roast, lettuce, a slice of tomato, cheese, it was a thing of beauty! And the bread! Thick slices of white bread that looked soft as a pillow.

I looked up at him, surprised. "Is that homemade bread?"

He pretended to look hurt. "What? A man can't bake his own bread?"

I tilted my head giving him a look. "Of course he can. I just didn't think you were the baking type."

"I'll have you know there's a lot you don't know about me, Princess. I'm just full of surprises!" He scooted the tray a bit closer to my lap. "Now eat."

I picked up a crisp and took a bite. They had salt and bbq seasoning on them and I immediately regretted it when they touched the cut on my lip. I took a sharp inhale then regretted that as well because pain shot through my bandaged torso.

"FUCK!" I cursed.

The expression on his face shifted through worry, amusement of my outburst, and guilt for giving me something that caused my lip to burn.

"Ah I'm sorry, love, I should have known those were a bad idea!"

I tried not to react to him calling me "love" but my heart fluttered a bit. I ignored the feeling and shrugged. "It's ok, I didn't think about it either."

I picked up the mug of tea and took a small sip. The heat felt good and comforting, the amount of milk and sugar was perfect for my tastes. I was about to comment on that when he spoke again.

"I hope the milk and sugar is ok. I just made it the same as mine, I should have asked first."

How did he keep doing that? It was like he was in my mind, knowing what I was thinking before I did. "I.. um... it's perfect, actually. Thank you."

He smiled shyly, an adorable look on such a large man. "I hope you like the roast, I made it for tonight's supper before Ma told me I was having supper with her and the family. So it's been in the fridge waiting."

I took a small bite, cautious of my lip, and let out a small moan. "Oh my god, that's delicious! How do you keep it so tender? Every time I try a roast, it always seems to get too tough."

He smiled, "Trade secrets. I'll let you in on it some day, maybe. Now eat. I'm going to go clean up, but just holler if you need anything, ok?"

My mouth full, I just nodded. He walked out of the room, and soon, I heard the sound of the shower. I was hungrier than I thought, and the sandwich was done in no time. I even tried again to eat a few of the BBQ crisps, opening my mouth extra wide to avoid my split lip. The tea had cooled enough that I could drink it in large gulps, enjoying the warmth and comfort of a good cuppa. When I was done, I pushed the tray away and sat in silence. I was still painfully aware that I was wearing nothing except Liam's t-shirt. I took stock of the multiple gauze pads and bandages on my body. I lifted my hand to gently touch the swollen flesh at my temple and winced.

"You're my little whore!"

I suddenly heard the man's voice in my head, and I jumped, causing pain to flow over me. I frantically looked around as if I expected him to be in the corner of the room. Satisfied that I was alone, I tried to remember to breathe. All of the memories of the alley flooded through my mind, and I felt sobs rising in my chest. Anxiety and panic seized me, and my breath came in short, quick bursts. I was getting lightheaded and could hear myself letting out cries with every wheeze.

Suddenly, Liam was there, his bare chest and arms still damp from his shower, his beard and hair dripping cool water on my knees. He knelt in front of me in his cotton sleep pants and put his hands on my shoulders, forcing me to look into his eyes.

"Look at me, Princess. You're safe! I've got you!"

My manic glances around the room slowed, and I settled my gaze onto his green eyes. The concern I saw helped calm me a bit, and I tried to force myself to slow my breathing.

"Tha's it, keep looking at me. You're safe here. I've got you."

All I could do was nod. The anxiety was settling, but sadness took over, and I just cried. Without thinking, I just leaned forward into his arms and sobbed into his chest. He held me gently, caressing my hair and murmuring, "I've got you, you're ok, you're safe."

We stayed like that for several minutes until my sobs eased. I felt exhausted from stress, fear, and pain. Before I realized what was happening, he had lifted me up into his arms and was carrying me down the hall. Carrying me as though I weighed nothing! He pushed open a door with his foot, and we were in his bedroom. He laid me down on the already turned-down bed, pulling the blankets over me. He sat on the edge of the bed and pushed my hair out of my eyes, taking my glasses from my face and setting them on the bedside table.

"I'm going to go get one of your pain pills. I'll be right back, ok?"

I squeaked out a small "Ok." as he rushed out of the room. Soon he was back with a glass of water and a pill in his hand. He sat down again and helped me sit up enough to take the medicine and swallow it down. Setting the glass next to my glasses, he guided me back down onto the pillow. He reached over me to take the extra pillow from the other side of the bed.

"I'll be on the couch if you need anything. Just call out and I'll be here."

He stood and turned to leave. I didn't know how to ask him for what I needed. I was terrified of being alone, but if I asked him to stay, what would he think? I didn't want to give him the wrong idea, and while the thought of lying in his arms had passed through my mind over the last several weeks, at the moment all I could think was I didn't want to be by myself because I knew that sleep would likely come with nightmares, flashbacks, and fear.

I called out just as he reached the door. "Liam?" I spoke softly, wondering if he would even hear me.

He turned back to me, questioningly.

I swallowed hard, not knowing how to say it. "I... can you... I mean, I don't..." A fresh tear rolled down my cheek.

"Do you want me to stay?"

There he was, in my mind again, knowing what I was thinking before I could say it. I nodded silently, relieved. He gave me a comforting look.

"Ok. Give me a second, I'll be right back."

I waited for him to return, and soon he was walking back into the room with a quilt over his arm. He put the pillow back on the empty side of the bed and spread out the quilt. Amazed, I watched as he lay down on top of the blankets I was under and pulled the quilt over himself. He could see the question in my eyes.

"It's only gentlemanly for me to sleep under a different blanket. I want you to be comfortable. I'll be here to keep you safe. Now, try to get settled as best ye can."

Gentlemanly? Did men who liked actually exist? I lay down, and he called out for his Alexa to turn off the light before he fluffed up the pillow under his head. I couldn't help myself; a giggle erupted from me.

"You use smart lights?" I laughed quietly.

"What kind of man do ye think I am? Yes, I have modern technology, I can bake bread, I even have indoor plumbing!" He grumbled as he got comfortable.

"I... I didn't mean that. I was just surprised," I stuttered, embarrassed.

He gently touched my chin and lifted my gaze to his in the dim moonlight. "I know, Princess. I was just teasing you. Now, do you want me to just be here or... do you need me to hold on to you to feel safe? Whatever ye need, I'm here. Just tell me."

I thought about it for a moment. The fear was still just under the surface, and the dark bedroom wasn't helping much to push it away. I'd never had a man ask me if I just needed to be held, but the thought was so comforting, I knew I would be able to sleep in his arms.

"Would you hold me?" I asked in a whisper.

"Aye, come 'ere." He reached to pull me close. I pressed my head against his chest, using his bicep as a pillow, and he wrapped his arms around me like a cocoon. I could hear his heart beating a steady rhythm as he softly rubbed my back. The terror slowly melted away, and I felt safe, maybe for the first time in my life. There was no expectation in the way he held me, no assumptions. He was just there, protecting me from the darkness surrounding us, the darkness in my own mind, and before I realized it, I was drifting off into a dreamless, deep sleep.

LIAM

He lay in the dark quietly but not sleeping. Sarah felt like such a fragile thing in his arms, and the only thing in his mind was the desire to protect her. The thought of what she had been through caused a white hot fire in his blood, and he had to force himself to stay calm and relaxed. Now was not the time to be angry; she needed him here to keep her safe. She needed to rest.

Her breathing was slow and steady against his chest, and he gently kissed the top of her head. This woman who his sister had made out to be some kind of wild, wicked woman but who had been so scared to stand up and sing in front of a crowd, who opened up to him at the restaurant, who had been consuming his every waking moment (and honestly several of his non-waking moments) over the past several weeks, was now here in his home broken and bruised. And she needed him. Something shifted deeper in his heart, and he knew that he would do anything to make sure she always felt safe from here on out. And when he found the bastard who did this to her? Anger flared again, and he made himself stay still, arms wrapped tightly around Sarah as she slept.

Not yet. But I will find that mother fucker and he will pay.

SARAH

I woke to the sound of voices. I turned to see that I was alone in the bedroom, sunlight streaming through the curtains. I reached over to grab my glasses, wincing from the pain in my chest and the tenderness in my stomach. There was another pain pill sitting next to the water glass and a small note in surprisingly beautiful sprawling script.

"Take this as soon as you wake, keep the pain under control."

It took me a few moments to get into a sitting position, but I was finally able to get up enough to take the pill and look at my surroundings. The room was clean and sparse, a simple dresser, a rocking chair in the corner, the bed and nightstand, very minimalistic. On the wall across from the bed was one framed painting, Van Gogh's Great Peacock Moth. It was one of my favorite Van Gogh paintings, and I was pleasantly surprised to see it hanging on his wall.

The voices grew louder from the front room.

"You brought her here?"

"Of course I did. Where was I supposed to take her? I couldn't just leave her there!"

"No, of course not, but you should have taken her to the hospital, or called the police!"

"Cara, she asked me not to. I made a promise." Liam said calmly.

"Promise? She was attacked, Liam. It needs to be reported!"

"She asked me not to." His simple reply put an end to the discussion.

I stood on shaky legs and slowly walked toward them, Liam's t-shirt falling past my knees. When they saw me standing in the hallway, Liam gave me a small smile and came to help me the rest of the way to the couch. Cara's eyes widened with horror as she took in my head and bandaged, covered legs. Liam patted me on the shoulder and left us to go into the kitchen to make me some breakfast.

"Oh my god!" She rushed over to me. "Sarah, oh my god..."

"I'm ok, mostly. A bit sore. I probably look worse than I am, honestly."

"Sarah, I'm so sorry. I didn't know!" Cara's eyes filled with tears. "I thought it was just a prank. If I had known..." Her voice trailed off.

I shook my head. "You couldn't have known. It's not your fault. It's not as though I was telling anyone about the packages."

"How long has this been happening? Why didn't you say anything?" Cara questioned me.

I just shrugged. "He said not to. I thought he was just a creep at first. It started off as flowers, a stuffed animal, and chocolates. It seemed weird but harmless in the beginning. Then the gifts got stranger after a while: lingerie, lube, even a box of tampons once. It stopped completely for a couple of weeks. I thought it was over. Then I got the one you saw at work. When I left the office that day, there was another box at my door when I got home."

"What was in that one?" Cara frowned.

I hesitated, "Uh... it was a... a whip."

Liam let out a low, menacing growl from the kitchen, but didn't say a word.

"Oh god, gal!" Cara cried. "Why don't you go to the police?"

I shook my head vehemently. "No, no police!"

"Why the fuck not?"

I leveled my gaze at her, decided to be honest. "Because he said he would kill me next time if I did."

Cara gasped, and there was the sound of glass shattering in the kitchen. She jumped up and ran in to check on Liam.

"I'm fine," he muttered. "I just dropped the mug."

I could hear the sounds of them sweeping up the broken mug, sharing a quiet conversation that I couldn't make out. Soon, Liam brought me a plate of scrambled eggs, bacon, buttered toast, and a cuppa.

"Eat something, love. You need to get some food in your belly with those meds." He gave me a look. "You did that pill I left out for you, didn't ye?"

I nodded.

"Good girl."

My stomach fluttered again at his words. I tried to keep the feeling inside and not let it show that those words affected me so much. There was something about being called a good girl that did things to me that I didn't want to explain. Liam didn't notice, but Cara did. She looked at me, up to Liam, and back to me with a soft and curious smile on her face.

"Well," she decided against mentioning her observation and went back to our earlier conversation. "I still think that you should report this. You can't just let it go."

"I can't. It's too risky." I said around a mouthful of toast.

"Did you get a look at his face? Do you recognize him?" Cara asked.

I froze. Of course I did. But how could I tell them that? Cara went to that pub all the time. She had to know the guy, maybe even think of him as a friend.

"Uh, no... it was too dark. I couldn't see his face."

Cara seemed to accept my words, but Liam frowned slightly. He could tell I was lying, but didn't say anything.

"Do you need anything? Can I bring you something?" Cara motioned to the t-shirt I was wearing. "Some clothes?"

The thought of having my own pajamas on sounded wonderful. "That would be great! Some comfy clothes, maybe a pair of jeans from the dresser. And..." I hesitated again, looking up at Liam. "My laptop? Could... could I work from here for a few days? I don't really feel like staying at my place."

"Of course, ye can!" Liam looked over at Cara. "But you're not to go to that flat. That fucker could be watching the place, and I'll not have anyone going over there but me, understand?"

Cara nodded. "Do you know how to pick out the right clothes for her?"

Liam sighed, "It's not like I haven't spent my life around women. I know what clothes look like!"

I looked up at him gratefully. "I left the back door to the alley open when I walked out. Number 4. If I haven't been robbed blind, my laptop should be on the table. My keys are hanging by the front door. If you could lock up behind you?"

He put a hand on my shoulder. "Anything you need, Princess." He looked at his sister. "You stay here with Sarah, and I'll be back as soon as I can."

We watched him don his black pea coat, grab a small rucksack from the coat closet, and walk out the door. Soon, the sound of his motorcycle cut through the quiet morning, and he was speeding off down the road. Cara turned back to me, her eyes finding mine with a knowing gaze.

"He's totally smitten." She said matter-of-factly.

"What? No, he's not. He's just being nice." I protested.

She shook her head. "Naw, I know my brother. He's a good man and does a lot of nice things for people, but I see how he looks at you. You've gotten under his skin!" A slow smile spread across her face. "I knew you two would be a good match!"

I flushed a bright red. Was she right? Could Liam actually have feelings for me? There was no way. He was too attractive; he couldn't actually want someone like me, could he?

Cara continued. "I had an inkling that he felt something, the way he rushed out of Ma's house last night to get to you."

I looked up at her sharply. "What? What are you talking about?"

She blushed. "I was telling my brothers about the box you got at the office. I still thought it was just a prank or something, and I was telling them the story about how Aislin and I opened it and how, after you left, I put it in my boot to get it out of the office so no one else would see it. He ran out and opened the box, found a note at the bottom, and put the pieces together. He left right then and there to go to you. I didn't know exactly where you lived, just the general neighborhood, but that was enough. He was gone before I could say much of anything. I guess that's how he was able to find you when he did, thank god."

It all suddenly made sense. That's how Liam had magically shown up at that moment and scared the man off. My heart melted a bit thinking that he had been so worried about me that he drove all the way across the city to try and find me. I was so grateful and in awe of his actions, I started to tear up.

"Oh, honey, don't cry!" Cara put her arm around me. "Trust me, having a man like Liam watching out for you, it's the best thing in the world! Unless you're his little sister, of course, then it's just a pain when he scares away all your boyfriends."

LIAM

S.E. WALKER

Liam was brooding as he rode into Inverness to Sarah's flat. He could tell by her expression that she wasn't honest when she said she didn't know who her attacker was, and while he didn't push the issue then, he was going to talk to her about it later. For now, he just wanted to focus on getting her the things she needed and getting back to her. He finally pulled up to her building and parked next to the alley where he had found her. Seeing it in the daylight didn't take his anger away from remembering how she had looked lying on the concrete.

Pushing the image away, he searched until he found number 4 and opened the unlocked door. He surveyed the room, trying to understand what he was seeing. There were flowers everywhere, some in the trash and some on her table and kitchen counter. He could see a pile of boxes, some open to reveal various sex toys, and he knew these must be the horrible gifts that the pervert had sent to her. Growling to himself, he walked into her bedroom to search for some clothes. What he saw when he opened the door stopped him in his tracks.

Her bed was a mess, the blanket was covered in what must have been every pair of underwear, bra, and bit of lingerie she owned, all crumbled as though someone had piled them up then rolled around on top of them. He immediately knew that that fucker had been in her flat after they left that night. Digging through a dresser drawer to find a couple of pajama sets, t-shirts, and a pair of jeans, he went to the table to pick up her laptop. The clothes were dropped to the floor when he saw the note lying on top of the computer.

"A little surprise for my whore when you get home. Just a taste of what's to COME."

He hesitated, not wanting to invade Sarah's privacy, but determined to see what had been left for her, he slowly sat down and opened the laptop. Once the screen turned on, he was relieved to see that there was no password. There was, however, an open window with a video waiting to be played. Already feeling furious, Liam pressed play and began to tremble with rage.

On the screen was a video of her attacker, too close to the webcam to see more than his chest down to his knees. He was holding a piece of her lingerie and rubbing it against himself, masturbating for the camera. There was no sound, no features that would identify the man, just the disgusting display. Liam slammed the laptop down and shoved it away from him. There was no way he was bringing that back to her and letting her see this.

This piece of shite was going to pay!

He picked up the pajamas and took her keys from the hook by the door, locking up behind him, and went back to his car. Looking around to make sure that there wasn't anyone parked nearby watching the building, he left and headed home. His anger was consuming him. he had felt mad at people before, gotten into more fights than he could count, but this was different. This was a righteous outrage that he knew would only be relieved by finding justice. He sat on his bike and picked up his phone to dial Declan.

His friend answered on the third ring. "Liam, mate, what's up!" Declan's voice rang with amusement.

"Declan, I need you."

Immediately serious, Declan's tone was somber. "What happened? What do you need?"

"We have a job to do. Last night, Sarah was... she was attacked."

"Attacked? What do you mean? Is she ok?"

"No. She will be, but the bastard beat her bloody, cracked ribs, and black eye. And he tried to... he almost... MOTHER FUCKER!" Liam slammed his fist onto his helmet, then picked it up, worried that he may have dented it.

Declan's voice reached through the anger. "I got you, brother. Do you know who the fucker is?"

"Not yet. She said she didn't see his face, but I can tell she's holding back. She's scared. Dec, he threatened to kill her if she spoke about it. He threatened the woman I..." Liam stopped himself from saying the next word.

"You ...what? You can say it, Liam. I know you feel for her, and that's ok. From what you told me, she got in your head and sounds like your heart, too. If that's true, let yourself feel it, mate. It's about time. And don't worry, I'll make some calls, get Murph and Freddy to meet me, and we'll start hunting this fecker down. You see what you can find out from her and the boys, and I will meet you at your place. We'll find him."

"Thanks, mate," Liam said quietly, trying not to think about what he almost said before. They ended the call and Liam kicked the motorcycle to life.

Why had he said that? It wasn't true, was it? He barely knew the woman! He'd never given any credence to the idea of love at first sight; that was just bull shit romance novel stuff. But remembering the way she looked when she was singing that night, the fire in her eyes when she talked to him before leaving the pub, and the way she so casually talked about her past as if it was something she was just used to going through. Then the pleading look she gave him when he found her last night... It had all crumbled the walls he had built around his heart over the last nine years.

The way she had felt in his arms, holding her till she stopped trembling and fell asleep, twisted something in his guts. The smell of her hair as he kissed the top of her head, the way she had placed her hand on his chest as they lay there. He'd never felt anything like that, and he knew without a doubt that he wanted to hold her like that every night. He also knew that he would do whatever it took to protect her and keep her safe. And the cunt who hurt her was going to pay.

SARAH

Cara didn't really press me for more after Liam left us. We just sat together and chatted about nothing. Eventually, she turned on the TV, and we watched an old season of Would I Lie to You to make me laugh. While I still felt on edge, the show did lift my spirits, and I found myself giggling uncontrollably. When we heard the roar of Liam's motorcycle returning, I was starting to feel better, although the pain meds were making me a little groggy.

Liam walked into the house and handed me the rucksack with my clothes. "Cara, you'll need to run into town and buy her some knickers. I would have stopped on my way, but I don't know the size."

I frowned. "My underwear was all in the drawers. You couldn't find any?" Realizing that it might have been too embarrassing for him to pick out my underwear, I blushed. "Sorry, I get it. I shouldn't have assumed that you'd grab those for me."

Shaking his head, he stopped me. "Naw, it wasn't that. I... I'll tell you later." Turning back to his sister, he handed her his bank card. "Go get what she needs, anything." Giving me a quick glance and a slight grin, he continued. "And pick up whatever chocolates she likes."

How did he know I needed chocolate?

Cara looked at me, waiting. I stammered, trying to think. "Um... a mint Aero? Maybe Cadbury Dairy Milk?"

Liam laughed, "That's it? Have ye not tried anything but the vending machine shite?" He looked back at Cara. "Pick up some Mackie's too."

Giving us a knowing look, Cara just smiled and left. I turned to Liam questioningly. "Was everything there? Did someone rob me while the door was unlocked?"

His expression darkening, he shook his head. "Not robbed. But... I think that fucker was in your place after we left. No, I know he was. That's why I didn't bring your laptop." He sat down and took my hand. "I don't know how to tell you this delicately. It looked like he took all your... intimate clothes... and piled them on the bed. I didn't look too closely, but I think he was lying on them. And he recorded himself using your webcam."

"What?! What was he doing?"

Fire flashed in Liam's eyes. "I don't think you want to know."

I stared at him, feeling my own anger rising. "Tell me," I said flatly.

After a moment, he responded. "He had a pair of your knickers. He was... pleasuring himself with them."

Rage boiled inside my chest. Despite processing the violation of my own body, somehow, in that moment, knowing that this pervert had been in my home, my sacred space, felt even worse.

"That dirty cock sucker! How dare he go into my home and jerk off with my underwear!! I'll kill him!"

Something like amusement mixed with pride crossed Liam's face. "Aye, that's how I feel about it, too, love."

I stood on shaky legs and paced the living room. "This bastard has stalked me, sent me horrible gifts, called me vile names, beat the shit out of me, almost ra... I mean, almost..." I couldn't make myself say the word. "And now he's getting off on camera, in MY home with my PANTIES??"

"I know, love." He stood to block my path and make me face him. "I know you're angry. I am, too. But I also know that you were lying earlier. You know who he is, don't you?"

I stared at him, frightened and in awe of this hulk of a man who had an eerie way of reading my mind. "No... I mean, I don't really know him."

"Don't play games, Princess. You know what I mean. You recognized him, didn't you?"

"Liam, I... I can't!" Teas began flowing down my cheeks. "He said he'd kill me, and kill whoever I told. I can't risk that. I can't let him hurt you!" I blurted that last part out before I realized what I was saying. But I knew it was true. I couldn't take a chance that this bastard would hurt Liam.

His gaze softened. "Ah, Princess, you don't have to worry about me. I can handle myself. Besides," he looked out the window to see a truck pulling up to the house. "My boys have my back!"

I turned and looked out to see three men getting out of the truck. Glancing back at Liam, I gave him a puzzled look. "Who are they?"

He bent down to pull a pair of my pajama shorts out of the bag and handed them to me. "Best cover up a bit better before the boys come in, Princess. These are my best mates, my brothers. They're going to help me find the fucker who did this to you."

Stunned, I slowly pulled on my soft pants and stared, my mind spinning. They were going to find him? For me? No one had ever been defensive of me before, not like this. The idea that Liam wanted to go after this guy, avenge me, made something churn in my stomach. And if I'm honest, in my heart.

I watched the men walk into the house, each of them so different, yet it was clear that they had a strong bond. They each embraced Liam and stood off to the side until introductions were made. I could see how all of them hesitated, taking in the lump on my temple and bandages with a mixture of sadness and outrage. Liam gestured to a stout man with black hair.

"Sarah, this is Declan. He's been my best mate since we were practically babes in nappies. And this," he pointed to a man almost as tall as him with white blonde hair and startlingly blue eyes, "Is Murph. And of course, Freddy here." The last man was only a few inches taller than me, but sturdy and intimidating. Bright red hair framed his face and bushy beard. All of the men had arms covered in tattoos. At first glance, they might have seemed like the type you wouldn't want to come across alone at night, but there was something in their eyes, a kindness that was now extending towards me.

"Hello," I whispered. I still wasn't exactly sure what was happening, what Liam had planned.

Declan reached out a hand to me. "Halo! Pleased to meet you. I'm... I'm sorry about... about what happened. Any man who would do that to a woman, well, he's no' really a man."

"Aye, you just tell us who he is, lass, we'll handle 'im." Murph piped up.

I looked from one man to the next, finally setting my gaze on Liam. What was going on? This felt like something out of a movie; men like this weren't real. These were total strangers to me, yet they were ready and willing to track down my attacker... why?

"We were just discussing that," Liam said. "She was just about to tell me who it was." He gave me a pointed look.

I sat back down on the couch and sighed deeply. "I can't, Liam! What if he comes back? He said he would kill me and whoever I told, he said... he... said he would make them watch while he... finished what he started." I buried my face in my hands and cried.

I could hear those men muttering quietly among themselves. It almost sounded like they were growling. Then I felt Liam sit down beside me and place a hand gently on my back.

"I know yer scared. But he won't find ye, not out here. There's no way he knows where ya are. And as for him doing anything to us?" Liam laughed bitterly. "He doesn't stand a chance. Just tell us who he is, and we'll take care of it. You'll be safe, Princess, I swear."

"Aye, we know how to deal with scum like that. No one will get to you." Freddy said quietly.

I looked up at Liam with tear-filled eyes. "The DJ," I finally whispered.

It took him a moment to register what I said. "From the pub? The night we met?" I could see him putting the pieces together, remembering that night when the DJ interrupted our conversation at the bar.

I nodded. "He must have taken my name from the sign-up sheet and used it to find me. He started sending me all those stupid gifts. And that night... he said he knew I was singing to him. I... I swear I wasn't!" Another round of sobs shook my body, and Liam gathered me into his arms.

"I know you weren't, love. He's just sick in the head." He turned to his brothers. "I don't know his name, but check with the manager at the pub, find out who DJs for their karaoke nights."

With a nod, they left on their mission, and Liam just held me, gently rubbing circles on my back and muttering comforting words into my hair. I felt the tension start to drain away, and I found myself leaning into him more, pressing my cheek tight against his heartbeat. I wound an arm around his waist and clung to him. He smelled like coffee, cologne, and leather. I raised my head slightly, not realizing what I was doing, and took in a breath against his neck, savoring the scent of him and the safety of his arms. I felt his heart rate speed up and his body go still. His embrace tightened slightly, and on instinct, I nuzzled into his neck, my free arm reaching up to wrap around his shoulder.

"Mo chridhe," he murmured.

I leaned back to look into his eyes. "What does that mean?"

The look in his eyes was something I couldn't interpret, but it sent a chill down my spine. Instead of answering my question, he asked one of his own.

"Do ye feel up for a little stroll?"

Startled by the abrupt change, I nodded. My painkillers had taken away most of the extreme pain. The worst part was my ribs, but the tight wrap was keeping them from causing too many issues. I could probably take a little walk, and the fresh air would do me some good.

He stood and got a heavy flannel coat out of the closet, the rich blue and green plaid blending together in almost a teal. He draped it over my shoulders and gave me a pair of boots that were a million sizes too big. He laughed when I put my feet into them, looking like a kid wearing her father's boots in a coat that reached my knees.

"Tha thu cho bheag!"

I gave him my best eye roll. "You're going to have to stop speaking Gaelic if you won't tell me what it means."

He chuckled, "It means you're just a wee thing!"

No one had ever called me a wee thing; usually, it was the opposite. I was made fun of for my size all my life, never described as anything close to small. Even when I lost weight, I was considered "big" or "plus-sized" by everyone, especially men. My ex would tell me he liked my curves, but then would cheat on me with someone half my size. This man must be blind to think I'm small!

He opened up the front door and took my arm, leading me outside. The sun was shining brightly, but I could tell that it was just starting to push back a heavy mist. We strolled down the road for a bit until we reached a trail leading off into the trees. Liam helped me down the stone steps until I was on the flat path, and suddenly we were out of the trees. What I saw took my breath away!

"Is that...?" I grabbed his arm.

"Aye, that's Loch Ness. Drumnadrochit is on the coast. I thought you might like to see the view."

I stood in awe at one of the places I had dreamed of seeing all my life. The distant shore was still clouded in mist, but the early afternoon sun was reflecting off the water like a million dancing diamonds. Everywhere I looked, things were vivid green, and the air coming off the water made me grateful for the coat. Overwhelmed, I felt a tear escape down my cheek and I took Liam's hand tightly.

"Thank you," I whispered.

"No need ta thank me, Princess. It's just a loch."

"You don't understand. I made a promise to myself when I was a girl that I would see Loch Ness someday. Every other dream I had was nothing compared to this. When my ex would smoke away our grocery money and our electricity would get shut off, or he would have a really bad day and take it out on me, I would lay awake at night and dream of this place. The thought of coming here kept me going on some of my toughest days and... here it is!"

Liam wrapped his arms around me, "I dinnae know that. I'm glad I could bring you here, that it means so much to ye."

I gazed up at him, "It means everything! All you've already done for me, saving me, looking out for me, after all the stupid things I said to you that night at the pub. I don't deserve all this."

He placed his hand on my cheek. "Stop right there, love. You deserve this and so much more. I was a complete arsehole to you that first night, ya know. I thought I needed to be someone who talked like that, trying to make a good impression based on the stories I'd heard about you and your supposedly wild past. I was an eejit and I never should have said what I did. You were right to clap back at me. In fact, it was quite impressive to see you stand up for yerself like that."

I shook my head in disbelief, "I thought you hated me after that."

"Ach, no. As soon as you spoke up like you did, I knew you were something special. Then when we talked that day at lunch, I could see how strong you are, how much of an incredible woman you are. As a matter of fact," he pulled me a little closer to him, "I haven't been able to stop thinking about you since then."

"Is that... is that why you tried to come find me?"

Liam looked at me with a soft smile laced with pain. "Aye, my gut was tellin' me ye needed my help. For all I knew, even after we talked, you might still think I was an 'ignorant asshole' but somehow I just knew that you were in danger, that you needed me." His voice was low and gentle, his words meant for my ears only.

"When I saw ye there, in the alley, I'd never felt more scared in all my life. I thought I was too late. Then I saw you move and I knew you were still alive. My gods, Sarah, I thought my heart was going to shatter when I saw what he had done to ye."

I gazed into the eyes of this man who had done so much for me, protected me, cared for me, and who had only known me for such a sort time. How could his eyes make me feel so safe, his embrace make me feel not only secure but also give me butterflies. I'd only just met him and yet there was something about him that felt so familiar, like I'd known him all my life... and maybe a few lives before this one.

"Fookin' hell, I really want to kiss you now," Liam laughed

ruefully. "But I promise, I will never do anything that would make you feel uncomfortable, especially not with everything you've been through. Just know... I want to. You're beautiful, Princess."

I blushed a deep red and smiled. I usually didn't believe it when people said that to me, but there was something in his eyes that made me trust that he was being honest. He really thought I was beautiful, despite my injuries and bruises.

"Liam, I... I want to kiss you, too." I admitted. "I thought about what it would be like to kiss you that first night at the pub, I thought you were so hot and at first I thought you were Cara's boyfriend and I tried to make myself stop staring at you, but then she said you were her brother and I started wondering what it would feel like to kiss you, and then I wondered if you already had a girlfriend..."

He stopped my rambling by putting a finger on my lips. The arm around my waist tightened more, his hand moved to caress the side of my face, and his expression became more intense.

"Princess, shut up and let me kiss ye now."

I shut up.

Liam leaned in slowly, his lips gently caressing my forehead, my cheek, then down to my lips. He was careful to avoid the side with the cut, and his kisses were soft and sweet, like a feather barely touching my skin. I wrapped my arms around his neck and kissed him back. Fuck the split lip, I wanted to kiss this man!

His hand was still on my cheek, but he moved it back to entangle his fingers in my hair. As I deepened the kiss, I could hear a low moan rumble in his chest. I ever so slowly ran my tongue over his lips, letting him know I wanted more. His lips parted, and suddenly it felt like he was devouring me, breathing in my soul. I couldn't feel the ground beneath my feet or the wind coming in off the loch. All I felt was him.

LIAM

S.E. WALKER

They walked back to his house in each other's arms, not just because they wanted to feel close, but because Sarah was feeling tired from being on her feet for so long. They had made it halfway back when he could tell that she was too exhausted to finish the walk. Without a word, he bent down and lifted her into his arms. She was shocked, but when she realized that he had no problems carrying her, she settled into his arms and rested her forehead against his neck.

He sighed contentedly. This felt so right, so natural. The feeling of her against his chest felt like something he'd known all his life. And that kiss? It was like a familiar memory flooding back into his mind, and at the same time, the electricity and passion felt new and almost otherworldly.

As they approached the house, Cara was just pulling back into the drive. When she saw her brother carrying Sarah, she jumped out and ran toward them.

"What happened? Is she ok?"

Liam just grinned, and Sarah raised her head to look at her friend.

"Oh, everything is fine!" Sarah smiled shyly.

Cara looked back and forth between them, then laughed and shook her head. "I knew it! I fookin' knew it!"

"Alrigh' now, stop yer boasting. So you were right this once. Took ye how many tries before this?"

Cara waved Liam's comment away. "That doesn't matter. I was still right, you two are a perfect match!"

Liam just chuckled and carried Sarah into the house with Cara close behind. She had purchased new underwear, a pair of soft leggings, a sports bra, a pair of slip-on flats, a six-pack of IRN-BRU, and an entire bag of chocolates in all shapes and sizes.

"I also took the liberty of calling Mr. McLeod for you. Told him you were in a car accident and wouldn't be in for a few days. He said to take the time you needed, just let him know how things are going. Now you don't have to worry about work for a few days."

"Thank you, Cara, really." Sarah smiled and squeezed Cara's

hand.

Liam noticed Murph's truck pulling up, so he gave Sarah a quick kiss, popped his little sister on the back of the head affectionately, and left them to dig into the chocolates. When he got outside, Declan's face was grim.

"The manager wasn't much help. He only had a first name, Mickey. Apparently, this guy was just covering for the regular DJ who called in sick. Some Englishman who was in town for the weekend."

"Said he hasn't been back to the pub since. Couldn't give us much more than that," Freddy added.

Liam sighed gravely. "Fuck... we've got to find him. Well, come on inside and have a drink, lads. I appreciate you boys doing this for me."

Declan smiled. "That's what brothers are for, mate. Besides, I've seen how this lass looks at ye. If she feels even half of what it looks like she feels, I'll wager she'll be joining the family soon, and family watches out for one another."

The men all laughed at Liam's blush but noticed he didn't actually protest. Declan raised his eyebrow. "Am I right, Li?"

"I...ah dinnae ken. It's too soon to say anything for certain."

Murph chuckled. "That's all we needed to hear, brother. The fact that yer even thinkin' on it means it's true."

Liam ran his hands through his long hair and sighed. "Ah suppose yer right. I cannae explain it. It's like I've always known her. And seeing her like that last night..." His voice trailed off, and his fists clenched.

"Aye, I know," Declan said quietly. "Seein' how she looked today, I can only imagine. I felt ready to punch through this fucker's head, and I'm not in love with the gal."

Before Liam could respond to the word "love," the boys all laughed and pushed him towards the door.

"Come on, let's have that drink you offered, we'll order a take away and relax." Declan smiled. Tomorrow, we'll get to work on finding this whore's son."

The rest of the evening went exactly as Declan described.

Freddy picked up the order from Taste of China, and they spent the evening sharing cartons of food, drinking, and laughing over card games. Colin came by as well, with his wife, Isla, and everyone settled into their normal and comfortable routine. Liam kept a close eye on Sarah to make sure that the fun wasn't draining her too much. But despite her soreness and obvious headache, she still seemed to be enjoying herself.

As he lost another round of poker and had to hand over a fiver to Murph, Sarah came over to stand next to him, putting her arm across his shoulders. He leaned into her for a moment, treasuring her closeness. He angled his head up, inviting her in for a kiss, and felt a thrill when she didn't hesitate, leaning down to kiss him sweetly, naturally. After a split second, Freddy whistled and Declan cheered, causing Sarah to blush furiously, but she smiled. She reached toward the center of the table and picked up another prawn cracker. She waved to the table as she walked back to the couch to continue her game with Cara and Isla. The girls were playing for chocolates instead of money, and Sarah had a nice pile of sweets on her end of the sofa, obviously winning. The giggles coming from the couch warmed him to his core.

Liam kept glancing at Sarah, in awe of how she seemed to fit in with his family so well. He was pleased to see her laughing and joking with Isla and Cara, like sisters. It made something in his heart melt a little more at the thought of it, but it also made him even more determined to protect her and find the man who hurt her.

SARAH

Even though laughing hurt my ribs, it felt good too. I looked around the room at these people I had just met, but somehow felt like I already knew them. Their natural rhythm with each other felt familiar, the playful banter, the way they maneuvered around each other getting drinks and food, like it was almost a dance. It was a strange and new feeling, but it also felt like something my soul had been missing... a family.

"Hellooo, Sarah? It's your turn!" Isla's grin was infectious. Her curly red hair was a wild mess that reminded me of a true Highland queen. She had beautiful freckles splashed across her cheekbones and the most emerald green eyes that seemed to flicker with inner candlelight. But it was her spirit that drew me in the most. Obviously, Colin had told her what happened because she didn't react when she saw my bruised and swollen face. She simply gave me a quick hug like she'd known me for years and began chatting away, telling me stories of Liam and Colin as boys, as if she was trying to catch me up on the years I'd missed with the family.

I place my cards on the couch. "Full house, hand it over, ladies."

Cara and Isla groaned playfully and reluctantly gave me more of their chocolate. The boys finished their round of cards and Freddy declared that it was time for a toast to celebrate this little family. Everyone stood to grab a drink, and Colin gave me a stern look.

"Ye know it's not good to mix alcohol with painkillers, right?"

I gave him a look. "I know... but I haven't had anything so far tonight, and it's been six hours since I took my last pill. One shot won't hurt!"

"Aye, let her have a drink, my love!" Isla pressed her husband, knowing that she would win in the end. "After everything, she deserves it more than any of us!"

"Hear, hear!" Cara called out from the kitchen where she was pouring the shots. "One isn't going to hurt her!"

Knowing he was fighting a losing battle, Colin caved. "Fine,

fine... just one!" He said seriously, but with a hint of humor behind it.

We all gathered in the kitchen and raised our glasses high.

"To our brotherhood, both blood and choice!" Declan called out.

"To chosen family!" Murph echoed.

"And to Liam and Sarah!" Cara winked at me.

My cheeks burned, but I smiled shyly as everyone cheered in agreement. Liam gave me a look that I couldn't quite read, but it made my legs weak in the best way.

"Slàinte mhath!" was echoed across the room, and we all downed our shots.

The evening slowed down, and everyone settled into comfortable seats in the living room, the fire roaring warmly in the corner. Liam pulled a guitar from the coat closet to the delight of everyone. I gazed at him in amazement. What is there that this man couldn't do?

Liam's broad smile lit up the room. "I couldn't do without singing this one, just for you, Col and Isla!"

Everyone began cheering, and I just looked around, feeling the excitement but not knowing what to expect. Liam looked at me, reading my mind again.

"I sang this at their wedding. It's their song."

Before the first note was played, Colin and Isla were on their feet, ready to dance.

Liam's voice called out strong and loud, "Sooooo..."

He started a cheerful melody, stomping a drum beat with his foot as he played.

"We danced all night 'til the sun came up, one for the road and another for luck. I didn't know that I fell in love, in love with my Highland girl. Hair like fire and eyes like the sea. She danced with the wind and sings like the breeze. I didn't know, but now I can see I'm in love with my Highland girl!"

Isla laughed as Colin spun her around in a lively dance. Everyone was clapping along and smiling, and I couldn't help but clap along, caught up in the happy vibe. When the chorus started, everyone joined in loudly.

"La di di le di di, la di da, la di di le di di, la di da, la di di le di di, la di da, I'm in love with my Highland girl!"

I had never been around people who were so full of life and happy to be together. I just looked at everyone in awe. Colin and Isla were spinning in each other's arms, their love for each other radiating through the whole room. In the middle of the second verse, Murph grabbed Cara's hand and pulled her onto the floor, and they joined in the dance. I couldn't help but laugh because the joy was contagious.

"I walked to the bar and looked to my left. I tried to breathe, but you stole my breath. You turn away and played hard to get but darling the night is young. The band started playing my favorite song, and that's when I caught you singing along. Right then, I knew that you were the one, but darling, the night is young."

Liam looked like he was truly in his element, playing a song for the people he loved. When the chorus was sung for the last time, he stopped strumming and rapped out the beat on the side of the guitar. Everyone stopped dancing and clapped as loud as they could.

"La di di le di di, la di da, la di di le di di, la di da, la di di le di di, la di da, I'm in love with my Highland girl!"

When the song was over, cheers rang out while Colin kissed his bride passionately, playfully grabbing her backside. Cara sat down pretending to be out of breath while Murph plopped down next to her, kissing the top of her head affectionately.

My heart was still beating the rhythm of the song when Liam began to pluck a few random chords before he began the next song. I had no idea what to expect next, but I had no doubt that it was going to be incredible.

He began strumming softly. The tune sounded familiar, but I couldn't place it until he started singing. His voice was clear and strong as he began.

"When I was a young boy, my mother said to me, 'Find yerself a pretty lass, don't take her love for free.' From the fields of Aberfeldy to the shores of Loch Maree, I know that she's the only one for me."

The song flowed over me like a blanket, both because of the lyrics and the way his voice hit my heart. It was deep, like the ocean's undercurrent, and had a power to it, as if he was pulling colors from the very air around us and weaving them into the words. The purity of his song and his voice brought tears to my eyes.

When he got to the chorus, everyone once again joined in. I wanted to, but I didn't know all the words, so I just hummed along, never taking my eyes off Liam.

"Oh, my love said to me, 'Will you meet me by the sea? You can kiss me underneath the misty moon.' She is stunning, she is pretty, she's as warm as amber whiskey and as bonny as the heather on the hill."

I didn't realize I had been staring at him so intently until the last note faded and I could feel everyone's eyes on me. I laughed shyly and wiped the tears from my cheeks.

"Wow... that was amazing, Liam!"

Declan chuckled softly, and everyone smiled.

"Dinnae ya ken he could sing?" Freddy asked.

"No, I had no idea. It should have been you on stage that night for karaoke!" I said it before I realized it. Liam gave me a haunted look.

"I wish it had been. Then maybe..." He stopped, but I knew what he was thinking. Maybe that man wouldn't have noticed me and become so obsessed. Maybe none of this would have happened.

I put my hand on his arm. "Will you sing another song?" I wanted to take his mind off the dark thoughts and guilt he was feeling. There was no reason for him to feel guilty about anything. He was the reason I escaped when I did and was here, alive, right now.

He nodded, more to shake the thoughts from his head than in actual agreement. He put a capo on one of the frets and tested the strings to make sure they were exactly how he wanted them. At the first chord, the melody flowed around the room like smoke. Airy but dense, swirling chords around me and into my soul.

"*Oh, the summer time is comin', and the trees are sweetly bloomin', and the wild mountain thyme grows around the bloomin' heather. Will ye go, lassie, go?*"

No one joined in this time. It was as if we were all in a trance, or maybe it was just me. I couldn't move, couldn't breathe.

"*And we'll all go together to pull wild mountain thyme all around the bloomin' heather, will ye go, lassie, go?*"

His eyes locked onto mine as he sang the second verse.

"*I will build my love a bower by yon pure crystal fountain, and 'round it I will pile, all the wild flowers o' the mountain.*"

I forgot how to breathe as I watched him, the traditional song sounding new in his strong voice.

"*I will range through the wilds and the deep glen sae dreary; and return wi' their spoils, tae the bower o' my dearie. Will ye go, lassie, go?*"

In the brief moment before the next verse started, Liam's fingers played across the strings, pulling chords and harmonies out of the guitar like dreams. I had never heard anything as breathtakingly beautiful in my life. I felt like my heart was going to shatter, and I found myself trembling. No one had ever looked at me like the way Liam kept my gaze while he sang, especially not while singing such a beautiful song. I was mesmerized as he finished. The last strum seemed to echo around the room. Liam never took his eyes off me until Declan cleared his throat awkwardly.

"Well then, boys, I think that's our cue to go."

Startled, I looked up. Colin and Cara were grinning like fools, and Murph's shoulders were shaking with silent laughter. My cheeks flushed, and I swear Liam's did too. The group stood and gathered their things. There were lots of hugs and playful banter as they filed out the door.

Isla pulled me into her arms. "I'm so glad you're here, Sarah. I know it's under horrible circumstances, but..." She paused thoughtfully. "I think bad things happen sometimes in order to bring us into the place we're meant to be, to show us something, or to maybe allow something better to heal us. I think you're where you need to be. I'm not pushing anything on you, but just know, you're good for him."

She squeezed me tight again and took Colin's hand as they walked out to their car. I was standing there, still reeling from the song and now from Isla's words. Why did I find myself agreeing with her? How was it possible that I felt so at home here with these people... with him?

As Liam shut the door and turned the lock, I suddenly felt nervous. It wasn't in a fearful way, but a sense of something electric in the air and the unknown. In order to distract myself from this feeling, I began gathering up the plates and glasses to carry into the kitchen. Staying busy was good. As I set the pile of dishes in the sink, I felt Liam's presence behind me, like a wall of energy.

I turned slowly to face him. I let him see the anxiousness in my face, but also my trust. He brushed a strand of hair away from my glasses where it had gotten stuck and kissed my cheek softly. My breath caught in my chest, and my hands were trembling as I reached up and ran my hand over the braid at the nape of his neck. I let my fingers gently play across his shoulders, and he leaned down to press his face into my neck with a deep sigh.

"I promise, mo chridhe, I will never do anything that will make you uncomfortable or scared. I cannae lie, I want to carry you into that bedroom right now, but I won't. Not if you're not ready or don't want to. It's up to you."

That moment of vulnerability and strength of restraint in Liam pulled at my heart. He wanted me, but not before I was ready. He understood that I needed to be sure, especially after what I had been through, and it spoke volumes to his character and how his feelings truly were. This wasn't a moment of just wanting sex for him. He truly cared about how I felt and whether or not I would be able to express it.

"I'm not sure how to tell you what that means to me, Liam. No one has ever cared about my emotions like that."

He gave me a pained look. "Oh, Princess, you deserve that kind of care and more. You're not just something to be had; you're meant to be cherished and looked after. I..." he hesitated, unsure of how to say what was on his mind. "If you'll let me, I'll look after you, in every way that you deserve. I'll keep you safe, even if you never want to share my bed. I would never ask for more than you're ready to give."

I felt the walls around my heart, built so high and strong over the years, crumble into dust. He really meant that! It was up to me where things went, and he would still be there, watching over me. I put my hand on his cheek and smiled.

"Thank you," I whispered. "Thank you for giving me that space. I can't say how far I'm ready to go tonight, but..." I blushed. "I do want to share your bed with you." Before he could reply, I continued. "But first, I really need to take a shower!"

Liam laughed at the sudden ease in the sexual tension. "I'll do ye one better. Let me draw you a bath, and if you're comfortable with it, I'll wash your hair for ye, so you don't have to reach up and hurt yer ribs. No funny games, I swear. Unless you want me to," he added with a smirk.

I grinned and nodded. He left the kitchen to find a towel and start the water in the tub, while I pulled clothes from the bag that Cara had brought me. Not knowing how much I would need to put on after my bath, still unsure of where the night was heading, I just grabbed a t-shirt.

LIAM

His hands were trembling as he turned the tap on the bathtub. He had never felt a desire like this in all his life. It felt as though there had been an empty spot in his soul that knew Sarah was the missing piece. It was more than wanting to experience her body; he wanted her heart.

When the tub was full, he called for her. She walked into the room slowly, shyly, and Liam thought she had never looked more beautiful. She carefully pulled her pajama bottoms down, and he noticed her underwear went with his, and his heart skipped a beat.

Calm yerself, man. You promised, everything at her pace!"

"I... I think I need some help with the shirt and the bandage," she said quietly.

He stood to tower over her, helping her ease the shirt up and over her head. The wrap was still tight around her rib cage, and he carefully began to unwind it. She let out a breath when the last of it was undone.

"I know that helps my ribs, but god damn was that pressing down on the girls!"

He wanted to laugh, but the sight of the handprint on her breast stopped him, reminding him of how badly she had been hurt. He tried to hide the rage he felt inside as he helped her step into the tub. She slowly lowered herself into the water with his support, letting out a contented sigh of relief.

"Oh god, that feels amazing!"

"I'm glad you like it," Liam smiled. He picked up the washcloth he had taken from the linen closet and poured a bit of his body wash on it. "I'm afraid this is all I have. You'll have to smell like me until we can get you something that smells prettier."

Sarah laughed. "I don't mind. If that's what you use, I think it makes you smell good! As long as you don't mind me smelling like a man," she teased.

Liam gave her a playful wink. "I dinnae think I'll have trouble seeing you as anything but the beautiful woman you are, Princess."

He was pleased at the blush that comment sent across her cheeks. He lathered up the washcloth and began to gently swirl it over Sarah's back. He let her wash her chest, legs, and other areas while he reached for the shampoo. Using a large plastic glass, he poured water over her hair, then rubbed the shampoo in, massaging her scalp. When she moaned at how good it felt, he found himself hardening inside his jeans and tried once again to calm himself.

When the shampoo had been rinsed out and she had soaked for a while, he helped her stand and wrapped her in a large fluffy towel. Grabbing his comb from the shelf, he slowly began to run it through her hair while she sat on the lid of the toilet. Finally satisfied that he had gotten out all the tangles, he helped her dry off her legs so she wouldn't have to bend down to reach them, and then reached for her clothes, noticing that she hadn't brought anything more than a t-shirt.

"Is this all you're going to wear, love?" he smiled at her.

"Actually," she said slowly, "I think you can just leave that there for now."

His heart stopped. Was she saying what he thought she was saying?

"Sarah, are you sure?" He had to know without a doubt that this was what she wanted. He wouldn't risk her feeling like he had pressured her in any way.

She took his hand in hers. "Yes, Liam. Let's go to the bedroom."

SARAH

I actually surprised myself when I said that to him. Not that I didn't want it, but I usually wasn't that bold. But with him, I felt so safe and cared for, and I needed him to know that I meant every bit of it. He needed that reassurance as much as I needed to know he would stop if I asked him to, to know he was aware of my emotions in this moment.

Without saying a word, he picked me up in his arms and carried me into his bedroom. It still amazed me every time he did that, like I weighed no more than a child. He carefully laid me down on the bed and walked around to the other side to crawl in next to me. I was still wrapped in a towel, and he was still fully dressed.

"This feels a bit uneven," I said, gesturing to his clothes.

He chuckled low in his chest. "I just wanted to take things one step at a time. You make the rules tonight, mo chridhe."

"You still haven't told me what that means," I said softly.

He brushed his fingertips across my collarbone, making me shudder. "It means My Heart."

"Oh," was all I could think to say, overwhelmed by the tenderness in his voice.

He smiled. "Do you want to get out of that towel?"

"Yes," I replied breathlessly. "But you still have all your clothes on."

"I do," his eyes glinted with mischief. "One thing at a time. If you'll indulge me, I would like to take a moment and just enjoy the view."

He pulled at the towel to untuck it and let it fall to my sides. His eyes traveled up and down my body as if he were trying to memorize every curve, every freckle. I felt more than just physically naked under his gaze, I felt more undone, like my soul were on display. As if reading the insecurities in my mind, he slowly placed his hand on my stomach.

"You're so beautiful," he whispered reverently.

I started to shake my head, disagreeing with him but he stopped me before I could say a word.

"You are beautiful, Sarah." His tone was firm, as if there was no questioning him.

I felt myself tearing up, my emotions getting the better of me. Never had I heard those words with that much feeling and sincerity behind them. For the first time, I actually believed it, I felt beautiful in this moment with him. As a tear slid down my cheek, he bent down to kiss it away.

His hand drifted to my hip as he leaned further, his upper body now above me, propped up on his arm. He was so careful not to put pressure on my ribs and it made my heart swell even more. I reached up to unbutton his shirt, but he stopped me.

"Are you truly sure about this? No doubts at all?"

I gazed up into those deep green eyes, finding the strength to say what was in my heart. "Liam, I want you."

Something flashed across his face, almost anguish but mixed with joy, like he had never heard those words. I realized that both of us had been hurt so badly and trust was difficult. To see him feel something so vulnerable and raw hit me to my core.

He moved off the bed to remove his shirt and jeans. He left his boxers on but I could see the hard length of him and it set my pulse racing. How long had it been since I felt like this? Years, at least, maybe never. He climbed back onto the bed and lay down beside me, his hand slowly caressing my arm. I reached out to trace my fingers along the outline of the tattoo of a dagger on his chest and I saw him shudder.

Leaning over, he kissed me, as gentle as he did the first time by the loch. I ran my fingers through his hair and pulled him deeper into the kiss, wanting to hear that soft moan he had made that day. He fulfilled that wish and more. His hand moved from my stomach to my breast, gently massaging, drawing a moan from my own throat.

I arched my back as his tongue explored my mouth, my pain forgotten. At that response, his hand moved again, drifting down, softly touching the sensitive skin of my inner thigh. My breath caught, and a chill ran through my body. The expectation of where else his fingers would go was almost more than I could take.

His kisses moved down my neck, across my collarbone, between my breasts. Then suddenly he was no longer above me; he had moved down to settle between my legs. I was shocked. I had never known a man who willingly wanted to do this.

"You don't have to do this, Liam," I began to protest.

"Princess... shut up and let me enjoy you."

I shut up.

He slowly, oh so slowly, kissed one thigh, then the other, back and forth as he got lower and lower. And then, suddenly, he was there. Kissing gently, softly, as if he were treasuring every moment. I let out a moan when his tongue hit my clit, electricity shooting through my body. He didn't stop, enjoying the fact that he was making me squirm. No matter how I tried to scoot away from the overwhelming pleasure, he had his arms wrapped around my thighs and kept sending waves across my core.

I lost track of time and space as he feasted on me. I had no idea that a man could be so gentle and yet so passionate, especially while doing what Liam was doing to me right now. I was whimpering and moaning with every flick of his tongue. When I felt his fingers gently probe into me, I couldn't hold back any longer; the pressure had built too high.

I cried out as the pleasure took over all my senses. My legs shook uncontrollably as I spasmed at his touch. Never in my life had I felt anything as intense as this! Seemingly pleased with himself, Liam rose from between my thighs and returned to his place beside me, pulling me into his arms.

"Was that to your liking, mo chridhe?" he chuckled.

"Uh... I... yeah." I couldn't speak at the moment.

He laughed again, caressing my hair. "Good. I quite enjoyed that myself. I'm going to have to do that again soon, if that's alright with you."

I could only nod. I wanted to return the favor, but I knew that my ribs and bruised legs would make it difficult. Still, I was more than willing to give it a try, though, so I pulled away to get onto my knees.

"What do ye think yer doin'?"

"I'm going to show you just how much I appreciated that!" I winked at him.

He frowned and pulled me back down onto my back. "This isn't a bartering system, love. I got just as much out of that as you did. I'll not have you hurting yourself just to try and please me because you feel like you have to. When you're healed up and you truly want to, IF you want to, then fine. But not like this, not with you hurt."

I stared at him, completely stunned. He actually meant it!

"I... I don't know what to say to that."

He kissed my shoulder. "Then don't say anything. And if you're aching, we can stop here. There's no pressure for more if you're not up to it."

The honesty and compassion he showed me were too much. I wanted this man like I'd never wanted anyone before. I entwined my fingers with his and looked into those emerald eyes.

"Liam, I want you to make love to me."

LIAM

At those words, something crumbled inside Liam. He had guarded himself against all emotional connections to anyone for so long, to hear her say that and know that she meant it was like a balm on his wounded heart. He no longer doubted her; he knew that she wanted him as much as he wanted her. And oh god, did he want her.

Without another word, he slid his boxers off and settled his body above hers, careful not to let his full weight rest on her. He leaned down and kissed her passionately, deeply, letting all his feelings flow into the kiss. Not taking his lips from hers, he positioned himself between her thighs, his tip just barely touching her. When she felt him there, she moaned and moved her hips as if trying to pull him in, and he knew he couldn't stand it any longer. Slowly, he began to slide into her.

Gods, she is tight!

He worked his way in slow movements, giving her time to adjust to him until finally he was fully buried in her warmth. That feeling alone was enough to take him to the edge, but he held himself back. He wanted to feel her join him.

Withdrawing almost completely, he pushed back into her, watching as she cried out his name and dug her fingernails into his shoulders. They moved together in a perfect rhythm, their hearts beating in time, the earth rolling beneath them as if saying, "Yes, this is where you're meant to be!"

Liam looked down at this beautiful woman who had stolen his heart, feeling her legs wrapped around him, feeling himself melting into her. He said it before he could stop himself. It just fell out, seeming like the most natural thing to say in that moment.

"I love you."

SARAH

S.E. WALKER

I couldn't breathe, couldn't see anything but the rolling storm in his eyes. I was filled with him; he was buried in me in a way I'd never felt before. The lovely pain of being stretched, but then ecstasy of feeling as though he was made to fit inside me. And in the midst of all that pleasure, he said it.

"I love you."

No teasing, no pretending, just pure truth. I could see it in his gaze. He wasn't just saying it because we were making love; he was making love to me because he truly felt it. It was a difference I never knew existed before. For the hundredth time since meeting him, I became overwhelmed by emotion, and tears began to fall.

I could tell that he was immediately concerned that he had said the wrong thing.

"I... I'm sorry, I shouldn't have..."

"Liam, I love you, too. Now shut up and kiss me."

He shut up.

LIAM

He woke before she did, the sun streaming in through the parted curtains, casting sunbeams over Sarah's sleeping form. She was breathtaking! Pulling his arm out from under her, he crawled out of bed and pulled on his boxers. He was shocked to see that it was almost noon!

Knowing that the boys would probably arrive soon to figure out their next moves in the plan to find Mickey, he quickly started making breakfast for Sarah. He found his legs a bit shaky after the workout he got last night, and was suddenly concerned that she would wake up in pain from all her injuries. Feeling guilty, he finished scrambling the eggs, put them on a plate with buttered toast, and retrieved one of her painkillers from the bottle. Pouring a glass of orange juice, he put it all on a tray and carried it to his sleeping princess.

She was already starting to stir when he walked in. Giving him a sleepy smile, she sat up slowly.

"Good morning." She grinned.

"Morning, love. I brought you a pain pill in case you were too sore from last night."

She stretched slowly, testing her muscles. "I am a bit sore, but not as bad as I thought. Other than sore in places I wasn't prepared for." She winked at him.

He quickly sat down and placed the tray of food next to her. "Did I hurt you?"

His genuine concern warmed her. "No, not like that. It's just... It's been a while, and you're... well... not what I'm used to." Her blush sent a flash of heat through his body.

"Ah... well... I'm glad that you enjoyed yourself, mo chridhe."

She pulled the tray onto her lap and began to eat, a thoughtful and somewhat worried look on her face. Liam was almost certain he knew what she was thinking, so when she raised her gaze to ask her question, he stopped her.

"Yes, love. I meant it. I truly do." He reached for her hand. "And... do you mean it too? It's ok if you don't, I understand."

"Liam, I meant every word." She shrugged. "I don't know how it happened so fast, but I do mean it. I... I love you."

For the first time in years, Liam found himself on the verge of tears. This broken angel came out of nowhere and found him, needed him, wanted him. She loved him! The words echoed in his mind, playing over and over again as he convinced himself that it was real.

"And I love you."

He was about to lean in for a kiss when there was a knock at the door. He groaned at the bad timing but jumped up to answer the knock, not hearing Sarah call out behind him.

"Um, Liam, maybe you should get dressed?"

Liam pulled the door open to see Declan, Murph, and Freddy waiting for him. They looked him up and down, from the boxers to the tousled hair. It only took a split second before they burst out in good natured laughter. Liam glanced down and realized the state he was in, embarrassed.

"I see you had a lovely evening, brother." Declan cackled. "Good for you!"

"It was... I mean it's not just..." Liam couldn't find the words. He didn't want them to think it was just something meaningless, something that happened in the moment.

The boys walked into the house and Declan put his hand on Liam's shoulder.

"I know, mate. I can see it in your eyes. I mean it, good for you. You deserve this happiness."

Grateful that his friend understood what he wasn't able to say, Liam just nodded. He ran into the bedroom to grab the jeans he had left on the floor, pulling them on in a hurry.

"I tried to tell you," Sarah giggled.

"Ach you didn't try hard enough, Princess." Liam teased. He gave her a quick kiss. "Enjoy your breakfast, and come out whenever your ready." He stopped at the door and turned back to give her a pointed look. "But be sure you put some clothes on yerself."

SARAH

I smiled to myself. I had to admit, seeing him walking around in just his boxers was a lovely sight, but he looked just as good in his jeans and no shirt. I took another bite of my breakfast and sighed. Hot damn, this man could cook!

I could hear the boys talking in low voices and I suddenly remembered why they were here, what they were planning. I felt a cold chill run down my spine. This was too dangerous! I didn't want anyone to get hurt. Well, I wanted one person to get hurt, which was their plan, but the risk of someone I cared about getting hurt just to protect me wasn't something I was sure I could handle.

I quickly got dressed and ran my fingers through my hair. I could tell that it was going every direction thanks to both laying down while it was wet and the late night escapades with Liam. Remembering the feeling of him, the way he filled me up, sent waves of pleasure through me, as though just the thought of it was enough to send me spiraling again.

"Focus, damn it. There's time for that later!" I whispered to myself.

I tried to act casual as I walked into the front room and greeted the boys. Murph's eye brows shot up and Declan snorted, trying to disguise it as a cough.

"Morning, lass. Nice hair! Sleep well?" He winked at me and I turned fifty shades of red. I wasn't the only one, as Liam tried to hide his blush as well. It only served to make the guys laugh harder until Liam growled playfully.

"That's enough ye eejits!"

Their chuckles still floated around the room as Liam tried to get them back on track. I listened as they discussed their plans.

"I talked to my mate who's a bartender at a club in Aberdeen. He's heard tell of some of the waitresses saying they've been attacked by someone who sounds like this Mickey bloke. A few pressed charges, but nothing would stick; no proof. He's very careful about not leaving evidence behind." Freddy stated grimly. "My mate says Mickey was there again last week, caused a bit of trouble, but nothing too bad. He mentioned that he was going home after a gig in Inverness. I can only assume that by home, he means back to England."

"I doubt he'd want to stay around here after what happened." Murph agreed. "Do we know what city he's from?"

Freddy nodded. "He's mentioned how popular he is in Manchester several times, name-dropping a few clubs that he claims beg him to grace them with his god-like talent."

Liam frowned. "If he has a gig here, when and where?"

Shaking his head, Freddy shrugged. "He didn't say. It's definitely not at the pub he was in before; they would have told me."

Declan finally spoke, "I doubt he had an actual gig. I would say that he was more than likely talking about... well, his plans for our girl, here."

That statement sent chills down my spine. If this guy had been in Aberdeen for a while, that would explain why the gifts stopped during those two peaceful weeks. Then he came back for me.

I turned to face the table where the men were sitting and asked the question that had been burning in my brain.

"Just what exactly are you planning to do with him?" I asked. "If you beat him up, which he totally deserves, what's to stop him from coming back when he's patched up? He'll find me eventually."

The men exchanged knowing looks, and Liam stood up to face me. Putting his hands on the sides of my face, he stared into my eyes with such intensity it took my breath away.

"He'll not come find ye. He won't get patched up from this. Ya ken?"

I couldn't speak for a moment. I gazed up at this man in awe and wonder. Was he really willing to do what he's saying? He's willing to... what? To kill for me? I had no idea how to respond to that! No one had ever cared for me enough to go to those extremes to keep me safe. It made my chest ache but also sent fear through my veins.

The men all agreed that they needed to make a few more calls to people they knew in Manchester before they drove down there, wanting to be sure they knew the exact time and place they could find Mickey. I stayed silent until they left. They were all preparing to risk so much. Why would they do this for me? I wasn't anyone special.

When we were alone again, Liam sat next to me on the couch. Seeing the look on my face, he wrapped his arms around me and held me close.

"It'll be alright, Princess."

"But what if it's not?" I pulled away from his embrace to look up at him. "This is too dangerous!"

"Ach, the boys and I will be fine. That bastard won't hurt us."

I shook my head. "I know you can take care of yourselves. But what if you get caught? Liam, to do something like this... don't become a killer for me. I'm not worth it!"

The mix of emotions that played over his face was confusing. Sorrow, guilt, anger, pain... and love. He led me to the couch and sat me down. Then he stared at the floor for what felt like an eternity before he lifted his gaze to me.

"I need to tell you something. First of all, don't ever say you're not worth it. Sarah, I would burn the entire world to the ground if it would keep you safe!"

My heart clenched as he continued.

"But you need to know... I've already killed to protect someone I love."

He spoke softly, fearfully. I couldn't find the words to say, so I just held his hand and waited for him to keep telling his story. I could see that he was afraid of how I might react, and to be honest, I didn't know how I would respond. In reality, I just met this guy. I didn't know anything about him! But my gut was telling me to hear him out, that I already knew deep down he was a good man.

He began slowly, telling me about how abusive his father was, the drunken beatings he would give to their mother. His hands shook as he told me about that last night, when he heard his mother scream, how his mother took the blame to protect him.

"In that moment, my Da was not my Da anymore. He was a stranger, an animal, who was going to kill my Ma. I'd never done anything like that before, of course, but I knew that I had to do it. There was no guilt; it was the right thing to do. The only thing. She would have been dead if I hadn't stepped in." His shoulder shook with emotion. "I stopped being a boy that night. I became the man of the house, taking on the responsibility of caring for my Ma and my brother and sister. And it was our secret to keep; only Colin knows. I think Declan has guessed, knowing me as long as he has and seeing how my Da was during those days, but I've never actually talked to him about it. You're the only other person I've told."

He looked at me with tear-filled eyes, feeling the full weight of his words and the chance he was taking by telling me everything. "If it scares you too much to still feel anything for me now, I understand. I won't try to argue with you if you want to leave. But just know, I'm still going to make sure he'll never hurt you or anyone else again, whether you stay with me or not."

I sat silently, letting his story roll through my mind, viewing it from every angle. While my initial reaction was shock and horror, I put myself into his shoes, into his mother's shoes. I knew what that fear was like. I remembered having thoughts of wishing I could take that final step and end the pain by ridding the world of the evil I had been married to. I had just always been too afraid.

Liam had been so young, taking on a burden like that in order to save his mother's life. He wasn't a killer, he was a savior, a warrior. He was the shield keeping his family secure. I turned his head to make him look at me.

"You were just a boy, and you did what you had to do. I can't imagine how hard it was for you to carry all of that for all these years. It says so much about the kind of man you are, to have such a heavy thing in your heart and to still be so caring and compassionate. You didn't let it destroy you, you turned it into strength."

Liam looked up at me with such fierce gratitude, I thought my heart would shatter.

"Thank you, mo chridhe."

"You don't have to thank me! You also don't have to go after this guy tonight. You've already made me feel safe. There's no need to do any more."

He shook his head. "No, he can't get away with what he's done, and he's not going to stop. He'll find another woman to torture and hurt; I can't let that happen. And he's got to pay for what he did to you."

I wanted to argue, but the steel in his eyes stopped any further protest. I understood why he felt this way, but something told me this was a different situation than what he had faced as a boy. Somehow, I knew this would change him in a way I wouldn't be able to help, but I loved him for wanting to go this far just for me.

Before either of us could say anything else, there was a knock at the door. Liam slowly stood and opened the door to see Colin standing there solemnly. As if he had been expecting to see his brother, Liam moved aside to let Colin into the front room.

"I... uh..." Colin stammered nervously. "Sarah, do ya mind if I speak to Liam alone for a moment?"

"Of course," I replied and walked back to the bedroom to give them some privacy. I felt slightly guilty, but I couldn't help but leave the door open a crack so I could hear their conversation.

"Declan told me you're planning on trying to find this guy. Liam, are ya out of yer mind?"

There was a brief silence before I heard Liam quietly say, "If it had been Isla, what would you do?"

Colin said nothing for a long time, and I wondered if maybe they'd taken their conversation outside. Finally, Colin spoke again.

"I get it. I truly do, brother. But this isn't like before. You're not a lad acting on instinct anymore. You're a grown man and this is premeditated!"

"Aye," Liam sighed deeply. "It is. But what else am I to do, Col?

Let him track her down and try it again? Or move on to another woman? You know I can't do that."

"What about the police?"

"Ah, ya know they don't do any good! There's been reports made from other women he's hurt and they can't pin anything on him, he walks every time! I'll no' let him keep getting away with this! I can't!"

I could hear footsteps as Colin paced the front room. "And I'm supposed to just pretend I know nothing about what's going to happen? What if you and the lads get caught? What happens then, Li?"

"I WON'T GET CAUGHT!" Liam yelled, rattling my bones. He took a deep breath. "I'm no' stupid, brother. I won't let that happen."

"Liam MacKay, you know as well as I do that you cannae guarantee anything! If you get yerself caught, or worse, you get yerself killed, what then? What am I supposed to tell Sarah? You want her to carry that guilt for the rest of her life, knowing you died to avenge her?"

Liam let out an anguished moan. I desperately wanted to run to him and hold him until that pain vanished. Colin's voice was hushed as he continued.

"She needs you here with her. I'm beggin' you, Liam. Please don't do this."

"Colin, I love you. But I'm tellin' ya now, go home. It's going to be alright. Just... just go home."

I heard Colin sniff, as if he were fighting tears. Nothing else was said, but I heard the quiet click of the door, and I knew that he had left. I felt like I would still be intruding if I walked back in there right now, so I just sat on the edge of the bed and waited. I agreed with Colin, at least for the most part. I didn't want anything to happen to Liam! There was a small part of me that was in shock that anyone would take such risks for me, and it gave me butterflies, but it didn't overwhelm the fear.

I looked up to see Liam standing in the bedroom doorway. "I'm assuming you heard all that?"

I nodded sheepishly.

"It's ok, love. I'm not going to hide anything from you." He sat next to me and took my hand. "I don't want you to worry. I've got this, I swear. I'm going to be ok, and so will you."

"Liam, please. Please don't risk this for me. Just let him leave, and you stay here. Stay with me." I begged.

I could see his resolve start to crumble for a split second when he heard my pleas. He pulled me into his arms and held me close. I clung to him like he might disappear if I let go.

"Mo chridhe, I will always be with you. But... I don't know how to explain this so that it makes sense." He sighed deeply. "I'm no' being a possessive asshole, but... I love you. You're... you're my woman. And he hurt what's mine. I won't let him get away with that."

I pulled away so I could look up at him, and I saw tears staining his cheeks. I had been told so many times that I belonged to someone else. My ex staked his claim on me every day. The man who attacked me said I was his, and it had terrified me. But the way Liam said it was different. It was as if he saw me as a treasure to protect, making an oath to always watch out for me rather than feeling like he owned me. I suddenly remembered something my mom had once told me.

Live life to the fullest, Sarah. When you find true love, be the strong woman I know you are. And when your love says with pride, "that's my woman," it will be the purest compliment you'll ever hear. That's when you'll know you've found your soulmate.

I had lived through the horrors of abuse and promised myself that I would never let anyone own me again, never let myself be submissive to another person. But looking at this man who was willing to risk his life for me, I knew this wasn't him being dominant. This was a primal protectiveness that filled my soul with strength.

But my inner doubt still made it hard for me to trust that his intentions were so pure and true.

"You really want me? I'm... I'm yours?"

LIAM

Hearing her fear and disbelief broke Liam. To see how badly her heart had been damaged by people who had lied and used her, taken her beautiful soul for granted. He couldn't stand to see that pain in her eyes. He knew that he had to be open and make sure that she no longer held any doubts about his feelings.

He cupped her face in his hands gently. "Sarah Calvin, you are the most amazing woman I've ever met. You're beyond beautiful, you are angelic, and you take my very breath away! And beyond the outer beauty, you have the soul of a warrior. Your strength is more than you can fully understand, but I see it. I know that you've been hurt, and it kills me. But I am in awe of you because you didn't let it break you. You are still a kind woman who carries so much light and spreads it to everyone you meet."

He could see her crumbling in his arms, overwhelmed with emotion. He wrapped his arms around her waist to hold her up.

"I know you doubt yourself, but I need you to listen to what I'm saying, and truly hear me, woman. I do not doubt you. No doubts about who you are as a person or about my feelings for you. I love you, more than I even thought was possible. I realize it happened fast, but I just know. And this is where I want you to hear my words and burn them into your heart. I don't just love you, I'm honored to call you mine. I'm proud to be the man you want, that you love. And I will shout it from the rooftops until the whole world knows that I have been given the greatest gift in all this bloody universe. Your love.

Sarah's sobs shook her body as he held her. She tried to lower her face, but he wouldn't let her look away from his eyes.

"No, look at me, mo chridhe. Get this through that gorgeously stubborn head of yours. I love you. I want you. I'm proud of you, proud to be with you. I'm proud to be yours."

Sarah couldn't stand it anymore and clung to him like he was the only thing keeping her upright. He held her, one hand on her back, one cradling her head, and let her cry. His sweet Sarah, the woman he never saw coming but now couldn't stand being without. He knew that this moment was life-changing for both of them. He was finally letting himself feel, opening himself up without fear. And she was finally seeing her worth. He could give her the assurance that she was deserving of more than just a casual love but a true love that could burn through all doubts and pain and heal the shattered pieces of her fragile heart.

SARAH

I don't think I'd ever cried so much. It felt like a release of all the years I had suffered and felt so unwanted. When my tears finally stopped, I realized that Liam was holding me a few inches off the ground, keeping me pressed close to his chest.

I reached up to put my arms around his neck, and he hoisted me up so I could wrap my legs around his waist. I kissed him with every ounce of the love I felt, pouring myself into him as if I could live the rest of my life inside his heart.

He pulled back slightly to whisper in my ear. "I've never needed anyone as much as I need you. I don't mean just your body, I mean all of you, forever."

"And I need you, Liam," I whispered back. "But right now, I want you, too. I want to feel you again. Please, Liam."

A low moan escaped his throat. "Ach, Princess, don't say things like that to me, you're driving me insane."

"Don't you want me too?"

He shook his head in disbelief. "Are ye mad, woman? Did ya not hear a word I just said? Of course I want you, in every way. I just have to make sure that you know I want more than sex. I have to know that you understand this isn't just about what you can give physically. I want your brilliant mind, your laughter, your smile. I want to be the one who makes you get that little wrinkle in your nose when you giggle. I want to be the man who makes you feel safe. If you said you never wanted to make love to me again, I'd still want to spend eternity making you happy."

I knew he meant every word. For the first time, I believed that I was loved, in all the ways I needed. I had never felt this comfortable with anyone before, and it lit a spark in my smile, knowing that I could truly be myself with no worry that it would be taken the wrong way.

"Oh, so you'd be happy to live without sex ever again?"

He gave me a serious look. "If that's what you wanted." A twinkle glinted in his eyes. "Of course, I'd be spending a lot of time with my right hand, but I'd manage."

I laughed wholeheartedly. "Well, it's a good thing that I don't think I can live without feeling you inside me again. I think you've ruined my abstinence record, Mr. MacKay. And I have to tell you, I don't think I can wait another minute."

His expression grew raw and intense. "Well then, Ms. Calvin. I'd better be sure I'm keeping up with you."

He carried me to the bed and laid me down on top of the quilt. I pulled my shorts down as I watched him unbuckle his belt and lower his jeans. I still wasn't used to seeing his naked body, but it was glorious. He may not have had a six pack, but the sturdy muscles were there. His biceps rippled as he held himself above me. I looked down to see him hard and ready, and a shiver went through me.

My breath caught as he leaned down to kiss my neck, gently biting my skin. His nips and kisses trailed down my chest before he took my right nipple in his mouth. I gasped at the sudden sensation, and I ran my fingers through his hair.

While I was distracted by his mouth, his fingers began exploring my body. Tracing lines across my stomach and hips, he was sending waves of pleasure through me. He reached down until his hand was under me and he massaged my ass. I felt his hips pressing against mine, so I spread my legs wider, inviting him in.

He moaned softly, and I could feel him pressed against me. I lowered one of my hands down to grip him, stroking gently. He let out a deep sigh and rested his head between my breasts as he let me touch him.

"See, you don't have to use your right hand anymore. You can use mine." I said softly, teasing him.

He gave a low chuckle. "Aye, that feels amazing, love. But I want more than just your hand."

"Good," I whispered. I lifted my hips and guided him to my opening. I needed him more than I ever thought possible. I was wet and ready for him, and he slid in easier this time. I gasped as I felt him fill me again. I brought my hands up to grab hold of his shoulders as he began moving in and out of my body, slowly at first. I knew he was being cautious because of my injuries, but in that moment, I needed more. I needed to feel just how much he wanted me.

I put my hand on his chin to make him look at me. "Liam, I won't break. I need you, please don't hold back."

He gave me a pained look. "I don't want to hurt you, love."

I smiled, "You won't." I let him see the fire in my eyes, my desire overflowing. "Fuck me, Liam."

LIAM

"Fuck me, Liam."

Those words lit a fire in his body. Still aware of her bruised body, he didn't let himself go completely, but he answered her desire. Feeling her tight around him was almost more than he could take.

He pushed his entire length into her, harder, fully buried inside her. He held himself there for a moment, enjoying feeling her wrapped around him. Then he pulled out and carefully rolled over until she was on top of him.

"Put me back inside you, Sarah. I want to watch you. Take control, love."

At his words, Sarah let out a moan and slowly impaled herself onto him until their hips were pressed tightly together, taking every inch of him. She began to roll her body, finding her own rhythm. He matched her and began to lift his hips so he could get even deeper as she used his body to pleasure herself. His hands gripped her thighs as she threw her head back in ecstasy. Gods, she was gorgeous!

Her movements grew faster, more frantic. She put her hands on his chest, her eyes closed as her face was lifted toward the ceiling. He could feel her orgasm building, and he wanted nothing more than to see her lose control.

"Look at me when you cum, mo chridhe. Let go."

Her eyes had trouble focusing, but she met his gaze as she rocked back and forth. Her nails dug into his chest, and she looked like she was fighting it, holding back to extend her pleasure.

Liam gripped her ass with one hand and put the other hand gently on her neck.

"Let go for me, my love."

Those words seemed to be all she needed to hear. Her body tightened around him even more, and she screamed as her orgasm spilled over her. Every inch of her body was shaking, and seeing her climax sent Liam over the edge.

He gripped her hips and drove her down onto him as he exploded inside her. Feeling his release sent a fresh wave of tremors through her, and she screamed his name as she came again. Liam's vision blurred, the world becoming a swirl of light and color. The room around them disappeared, and it was all he could do to remember how to breathe.

When he was finally able to focus, he saw her above him, chest heaving as she recovered, eyes closed but a smile on her face. He gently pulled her down to lie on his chest, still inside of her. When she made a small sound of pain from the way her rib cage was stretched, he immediately rolled over so she was lying on her side, but he couldn't bring himself to pull out of her. They lay there in each other's arms, spent and completely content.

SARAH

S.E. WALKER

I don't think I'd ever slept as soundly as I had in Liam's bed. No nightmares, no tossing and turning. Just deep, peaceful rest in his arms. And when the sun broke through the clouds and poured into the room, I opened my eyes to just stare at him lying next to me. His hair was undone and partially covering his face. I reached out to gently push it away from his eyes and looked in awe at his sleeping form.

He had one arm tucked under his pillow, the other slightly stretched out as if he were reaching for me in his sleep. All I could think was how beautiful he looked to me, and how lucky I was in this moment.

I rolled over onto my back and tried to process how I ended up here. Not just the fact that he had saved me after the attack, but also how I found myself falling for this man whom I had only known for a few months. In my past, I had always fallen for men quickly, which usually got me in trouble because I would overlook the red flags and let them manipulate my emotions.

But Liam never tried to tell me how to feel, what to say, or how to act. He seemed to want me to be nothing more than my true self, which was definitely a new experience for me. Even when he seemed to be inside my brain, hearing my thoughts before I could speak them, he was never pushy. It was as if he were a steady rock that I could lean on no matter how I felt. I'd never had that before. I had always been the rock for other people.

The circumstances that led me to him still seemed unreal. The random job offer in another country across the ocean to an office where his sister happened to work, the unusual decision to go out with Cara and Aislin that night, which was something I normally wouldn't have done... it was like the universe was guiding me to this moment. Even through the horror of that night in the alley, I not only survived, but I also avoided an even more tragic fate because of him.

I turned to look at him and saw that he was awake and watching me.

"Good morning," I smiled.

He stretched lazily and reached out to pull me close. "Good morning, Princess. Sleep well?"

I snuggled into his arms. "Better than ever."

Kissing the top of my head, he sighed contentedly. "That's what I like to hear."

"So what are the plans for today?" I asked. "Are the guys coming back over?"

"No, not until we hear something else. There's nothing we can do until we find out more information. So, since you don't have to go to work, we can do whatever we like today. What would you like to do?"

I pulled back so I could give him a cheeky grin. "You mean other than the obvious?" I reached around him to give his ass a light smack.

He has a hearty laugh. "That's my girl!"

A warm wave rolled through me at his words.

"If you want to stay in bed all day, we absolutely can," he continued. "But I was thinking maybe you would want to go into Inverness and see some of my favorite places. Besides, there's the Music Festival happening now. I thought you might like that."

"A music festival? That sounds amazing!" I sat up too quickly in my excitement and winced with the sharp pain in my ribs.

"Ah love, be careful. I want to take you but only if you feel like it."

"Oh I want to go for sure! Maybe I'll just take half a pain pill to take the edge off, since I assume you'll be driving?"

Liam winked. "I can drive, but I was wondering if you wanted to take the bike?"

I gave him a shocked look. "The bike? Really?"

"If you'd rather not, I..."

"I want to!!" I said quickly. "I've never actually been on a motorcycle before."

It was his turn to look shocked. "You're lyin'. You've never ridden a bike? Well that's something we'll have to remedy! Go get cleaned up and we'll head out as soon as you're ready."

I don't think I've ever showered as quickly as I did that

morning. Towel drying my hair, I grabbed the jeans that Liam brought from my flat, plain pink t-shirt, and the slip on shoes Cara bought for me. I studied my reflection in the mirror, assessing the bruise on my temple. It was still pretty ugly, but I was able to cover most of it with my hair. My lip was still healing but was no longer swollen. Considering everything, I looked almost normal.

Liam was drinking a cup of tea in the kitchen when I walked in and did a quick spin. "How do I look?"

He smiled warmly. "Gorgeous as always, love."

Out of habit from years of low self-esteem, I rolled my eyes. "Right."

He grabbed my hand before I could turn away. "I mean it, Sarah. Don't you know how beautiful you are to me?"

I shook my head and looked down. I wanted to believe it, but always being told I wasn't good enough, wasn't skinny enough or pretty enough, had taken it's toll on my ego. I knew he meant what he was saying but I didn't see it in myself.

"Look at me, Princess."

I raised my eyes to him, trying not to cry. I was so tired of crying. But this man had a way of making my emotions spill out of me.

He lifted my chin. "I want you to hear me now. You are more than beautiful. I thought so from the moment I saw you. You have the most amazing eyes, a smile that melts hearts and shows how much love there is in your soul. You've got killer curves, too. You are stunning, and I'm not saying that because I love you. It's just the truth. You need to know that deep down, don't ever doubt yourself."

I nodded, willing myself to take his words to heart. "I'm trying, Liam. Please don't get upset with me. It's just hard for me. I've never felt pretty."

His expression was pained. "I'm not upset with you, mo chridhe. I just want you to know the truth. I know that you've been torn down for so long. All I can do is promise that I will always tell you how gorgeous you are until you start to believe it.

And then I'll just keep telling you because it's simply a fact."

He gave me a tight hug, then handed me the giant plaid coat. As he pulled on his leather jacket, I stared at him in amazement. His thick frame filled out that coat so well! He had braided his hair again, and his jeans clung to his ass in a way that made me want to reach out and grab it. How did this man see such beauty in me when he could have any woman he wanted?

The early spring sun was shining brightly, and it felt unseasonably warm. Liam started up the motorcycle, and the low rumble of the engine made me shiver. I had always loved the sound of a bike! He handed me a spare helmet and I climbed on behind him, wrapping my arms around his waist. Soon we were speeding down the road toward Inverness.

I rested my head against his back and felt the wind rushing past me. This was the most thrilling feeling I'd ever experienced! I was in awe of the landscape rushing by us the entire ride. When we finally reached the city center, I was almost shaking with adrenaline. Liam parked the bike, and we began to stroll down the street looking at shops. We reached a doorway after a while, and Liam stopped me.

"This is one of the places I really wanted to show you." He put a hand over my eyes and guided me through the door. We took several steps before he removed his hand and let me look around.

"Surprise, mo chridhe."

I was speechless as I took in the view around me. I was surrounded by floor-to-ceiling bookshelves, not just on the main floor, but a second floor with a railing surrounded the cathedral-like ceiling. Books, books everywhere! I felt like Belle being shown the library for the first time.

I looked up at Liam, my eyes shining. "Oh my god, Liam!"

"Welcome to Leakey's Bookshop! It's one of my favorite spots in all of Inverness."

"This is incredible!" Unable to stop myself, I ran off to explore. I didn't know where to start, but it didn't matter because everywhere I looked, there were shelves and stacks of amazing books. I lost track of where Liam was as I wandered around in awe. The smell of books made me dizzy with happiness.

Soon he found me with my nose buried in a photography book filled with images of Egypt. He was carrying a basket, and I saw that several of the books I had picked up and admired were now nestled inside. He took the book of photographs from my hands and added it to the basket.

"Let's go to the cafe and get a coffee."

Speechless, all I could do was follow him. He pulled out a chair for me at one of the tables and walked over to the counter to order two lattes and a couple of pastries. When he brought the food over to the table, I gave him a beaming smile.

"This is the best date I've ever been on!"

He laughed. "Oh, the day is just starting, love. But I'm glad you're enjoying yerself. You'd better get used to this, ya know."

After we finished our breakfast, Liam purchased the books and we walked back out into the sunshine. A few streets down, we came upon a local band playing lively music. People were gathered around to listen, and a few couples were dancing.

Liam set the books down next to a tree and held his hand out to me.

"Care for a spin?"

I just stared at him. Was he for real? "I... I don't know." I didn't know how to admit this. "I've never actually danced, not like this."

He frowned. "Did ya never go to school dances or dance at a wedding?"

I shook my head. "No." This was so embarrassing.

He put his arm around my waist and pulled me to a more open area. "Then just hang on, lassie. I've got you."

I put my hands on his shoulders as he twirled me around. I barely had to follow his steps because he mostly held me close and kept my feet off the ground. I found myself laughing, my embarrassment gone.

The band ended the song and began a new one. I was

pleasantly surprised to hear a song that I knew. As the first verse started, he set me on the ground and held me as we swayed to the music.

I don't know if you can see the changes that have come over me. In these last few days, I've been afraid that I might drift away. So I've been telling old stories, singing songs that make me think about where I came from, and that's the reason why I seem so far away today...

As we danced in the center of the crowd, I realized I had never felt happier. And in the middle of all of those people, Liam pulled me closer.

"You look so damn beautiful, Sarah."

But let me tell you that I love you, that I think about you all the time...

He leaned down and kissed me deeply. Surprised, all I could do was kiss him back. I had never been with anyone who kissed me in public, as though they didn't care who saw us. But Liam let his affection show to anyone who cared to look. My knees went weak, and if his hand hadn't been on the small of my back, I might have ended up on the ground.

The rest of the afternoon was spent hand in hand, browsing through various stores, a local chocolate shop, then a light lunch at an outdoor cafe. I couldn't stop smiling and wondering how this was my life now. Occasionally, we would run into someone Liam knew, and he would put his arm around my shoulders and introduce me with a wide grin. He had said he was proud to be with me, and now I could see that he really meant it. He was showing me off like he'd won a prize.

The last shop we stopped at had a variety of scarves, hats, kilts, and blankets, all in the different clan tartans. They were all so beautiful, and I loved seeing the bright plaids. I was looking at a stack of wool blankets, admiring the quality and soft textures, when Liam tapped me on the shoulder and held out a bag to me.

"I got you a little something, Princess."

"Liam, you've already bought so much today! You didn't need

to get me anything else!"

"Hush now, love. Just let me spoil ya a bit!"

I laughed, shaking my head, and opened the bag. Inside was a scarf and pendant on a delicate
silver chain, both sporting a royal blue and green plaid. It was the same as the jacket he had given me to wear.

Liam blushed slightly. "It's the MacKay tartan. I wanted you to have a little piece of me, my
family's history."

Awed and honored, I studied the pendant. It was the clan crest, a hand holding a dagger and the
words "Manu Forti" along the top. It was the same dagger that was tattooed on his chest.

"What does that mean?" I asked.

"It means 'with a strong hand.'"

I stared at it in fascination. It seemed amazing to me how much the clan motto and crest so perfectly fit Liam as a man. His strength of character, his protectiveness, even the dagger fit his past so eerily. It wasn't violence, but a desire to take care of the people he loved.

"Will you help me put it on?"

Liam smiled sweetly and took the necklace from my hand. When I pulled my hair up, he placed
the chain around my neck and secured the clasp. I looked down at this incredible gift, overwhelmed by the thought he put into it. I spun around and wrapped him in a tight embrace.

"Thank you, Liam!"

He kept his arm around my shoulders as we walked back to his bike. After putting all the
purchases in the saddlebag, we headed back to his house. Once again, I breathlessly watched the world
speed by us, the sun just starting to creep towards the horizon.

The next few days were spent enjoying each other's company, sharing stories, and getting to know all those little details about each other. I had already spoken to my boss and arranged to use the sick time I'd built up. Liam still had to work, of course, so I spent time sitting on a chair in his garage watching him work on Declan's bike and an old farm truck that someone had brought in. I began to forget about everything that had happened, even my flat seemed like a distant memory. Life was so peaceful here with Liam, and I didn't want anything to change.

LIAM

Watching Sarah sit nearby while he worked made Liam feel more content than he could ever
remember feeling before. He would explain what he was working on, teaching her a bit about mechanics and the inner workings of engines. She never made him feel inadequate or inferior; instead, she asked genuine questions and paid attention to his every word. In the evenings, they would cook dinner together, laughing and dancing in the kitchen. Those days together were the happiest of his life.

Then, after almost a week of bliss, Declan stopped by with news of Mickey. Liam felt his heart
drop in his chest. He hadn't forgotten about getting justice for Sarah, but he had been enjoying the
peaceful days so much. His fear was that once Mickey was taken care of, Sarah would go back to her flat and her life, leaving him alone in the house that she had made feel like a true home. He didn't want that to end. Pushing those feelings aside, he sat down with Declan to hear what news he had found.

"I talked to my mate Luke in Manchester. Last week, his baby sister Lucy was at a club with some friends and met some guy who claimed to be a big DJ all around London. He tried to pick Lucy up, and when she turned him down, he slapped the shite out of her and tried to drag her into an alley. Luckily, the bouncer was on a smoke break and chased the guy off."

"Mac a' ghalla! Are we sure it's the same guy?"

Declan nodded. "Lucy told her brother that the guy's name was Mick or Mickey, and he said he'd been touring all around the UK at different clubs. From the way she described his looks, it sounds like a match to our man."

Sighing, Liam sat back in his chair. "Right, so do we know where he is now?"

"Well, before he went after Lucy, he was chattin' up her friend and mentioned that this weekend he was going to be at The Factory Floor. I had my mate check with the club to make sure that they had
booked Mickey, and they said he was supposed to be there Friday

and Saturday nights."

"Good." Liam stood and began to pace the room. "If his MO is the same, he may find some other woman to target the first night and might bail before Saturday, so we should find him Friday to be sure."

Sarah suddenly spoke up from the doorway. "Do you really have to do this?"

SARAH

Liam turned toward me, his righteous anger towards Mickey making him seem like a giant stuck in the small room. He took me by the hand and tried to smile reassuringly.

"I promised you that I would take care of you, that I would find this guy and make sure that he
never hurt you or anyone else again. I'm going to keep that promise, love."

I let go of his hand and wrapped my arms around my core, suddenly feeling cold. Liam was
looking at me like I was so fragile and he wanted to surround me like a blanket and keep me safe and
warm. I loved that look, but it still didn't shake the fear from my heart.

"And what happens if you find him? And you... You kill him? When it's done, what happens next? Won't you be worried that somehow it will get traced back to you?"

Declan cleared his throat. "Lass, we can get in and out of Manchester without anyone knowing we were there. It won't fall back on us, I swear." There was something in his face that told me he was putting on a brave front, but he was feeling the same nerves as I was about this whole situation.

Liam added, "And since you never reported what happened to you, there's no motive as far as
anyone is concerned that would tie us to Mickey. We'd be in the clear, nothing to worry about."

I nodded but didn't feel convinced. Declan could sense that he needed to give us some space, so he stood up, giving a promise to tell Murph and Freddy to get the van ready for them to leave tomorrow for Manchester. Before he walked out the door, he gave me a quick hug.

"Don't be scared, lass. I'll watch his back. I won't let him come to any harm," he whispered quietly. "But... try and talk some sense into him, yeah?"

I looked into his eyes and what I saw there told me everything I needed to know. He would support Liam no matter what, to the ends of the earth if that's what it took. But he did not want Liam to make this choice. He knew that the fallout would be more than Liam expected and was scared for him.

In that moment, I loved Declan for that loyalty. I didn't know everything that they had been through together, but it was obvious that these men were brothers, and Declan couldn't back out of this because he would never let Liam dive in on his own. I nodded my understanding and squeezed him tight.

"I will, thank you!" I whispered back.

LIAM

After closing the door behind Declan, Liam gently guided Sarah into the front room to sit on the

couch with him. He wanted to find a way to reassure her about everything, but he was dealing with his

own doubts. Not about tracking Mickey down, but what Sarah would do after it was over.

"Tell me what's on your mind, mo chridhe. What are you thinking? You can be honest with me."

Sarah shrugged. "I don't really know how to put it into words. You don't know how it feels to have someone willing to do this, go to this extreme, just to protect me. I've never had that before. That part of it makes me happy."

"But?" Liam pressed.

"But... if you do this... even if you don't get caught, will it change things? Will you change?"

He frowned. "How would I change?"

"I don't know... I love how strong you are and how you look out for the people in your life. And I know that the reason you're doing this is because of that protective part of your heart. You're like a guardian, and I love that. But... this feels different somehow. Colder? It's like Colin said, this isn't the same as when you were a kid; this is darker and planned ahead. That makes me worry."

Liam sat quietly processing her words before he replied. "Would it make you see me differently?"

Sarah looked at him, letting all her emotions fill her eyes. "I don't know, Liam. I love you, even

though that scares me."

"Why? Why are you scared of loving me?"

"Because it happened so fast. Because you came out of nowhere and suddenly filled up my life

with all these feelings and experiences I've never had. And because every time I love someone, they end up hurting me or leaving me. I promised myself that I would never let that happen to me again, but here I am, falling head over heels for you, and I'm terrified!"

"Oh love. I know how badly you've been hurt in your past. But I'm not like them. I'm not going to leave you, and I will NEVER hurt you like that. I'm not perfect, and I may be an arse sometimes. Maybe I'll say something stupid or accidentally hurt your feelings. It will never be intentional, and I will always own up to it and admit when I'm wrong. I want you to call me out on my shite and tell me when I'm being an arse so I can learn and be better... for you."

Sarah gave him a weak smile. "I know. And that kind of scares me too. Because it sounds too good to be true. Like you're not real and one of these days I'm just going to wake up to find this has all been a dream."

"Are you sayin' I'm your dream guy?" Liam winked at her playfully.

She swatted his shoulder lightly. "Ok, asshole, yeah, you're pretty much what I always dreamed I
would find." She grew more serious. "But what you're planning, that was never part of my dream. Being safe and protected by someone, sure. I've never known someone who... who killed someone before, not premeditated like this. And even though I understand why, even agree with you that it's what he deserves, for you to be the one to do it... I don't know how that will make me feel. I know I'd still love you. But I think I might be frightened of you, too."

That statement made Liam's heart sink like an anchor into the deepest ocean. The last thing he ever wanted was for her to be frightened of him, to compare him to all the people who had hurt her and were capable of that kind of violence. But he also knew that deep down, he couldn't let this go without finding justice for her. The two sides of his mind were tearing at each other viciously, and he tried to settle them before he spoke again.

Finally, he said, "I never want you to be afraid of me, my love. I need you to understand that just
because I'm ridding the world of that filth, it won't change who I am."

He meant those words as he spoke them, and inside, he

desperately hoped they were true. He didn't want to become someone different, someone more callous. How could he keep that from happening without letting Mickey get away unscathed? It was just a chance that he was willing to take; whatever happened would be worth it as long as Sarah was safe.

As if seeing the internal conflict, Sarah put her hand on his chest. "Liam, I know how badly you want to take care of me by doing this. But I promise, you don't need to. I already feel safe with you. He's not coming back here for me. It's over. Please, I'm asking you, begging you, don't do this!"

The pleading look in her eyes cut him to pieces, but it also reminded him of the night he found her in the alley and she had that same look, begging him not to take her to the hospital or call the police. The memory stoked the fire in his spirit, and he knew that he had to do this, no matter how much she asked him not to. He was doing this for her, and if this choice made her lose her feelings for him, he was willing to take that risk in order to make sure she was safe, even if that meant she wasn't with him when it was over.

"I'm sorry, Sarah." He said solemnly. "This is something I have to do. I'll deal with whatever happens afterward, but I'm not changing my mind. It needs to be done. If you decide after that you can't stay with me, I'll understand. It will tear me apart, but I'll accept it, as long as I know you're safe."

Sarah's eyes widened and filled with tears. "You'd choose this over keeping me?"

The heartache in her words was palpable. Liam's resolve almost broke then, but he couldn't let himself cave. His stubbornness overwhelmed his desire to comfort her. The fortress around his heart that had been slowly dissolving was being reinforced in self-preservation.

"I will always want to keep you with me. But if making sure you're safe means that you walk away, then I'll have to live with that. I'm going to find Mickey and end him for what he did to you. What you decide to do after that is up to you." His voice had a sharp edge to it, and he could see how those words cut her, but he couldn't take them back.

Sarah sat in silence, unsure of how to respond. Liam wanted to pull her into his arms and comfort her, but he felt as though he'd said and done too much already. In an effort to protect her, he'd pushed her away even though he felt it was for her own good.

I've got to get out of here before I hurt her anymore, Liam thought sadly. He stood slowly and took a step back.

"I... I need to go to Declan's and help him get ready. I'll give Isla a call and have her come stay
with you tonight so you're not alone."

He grabbed his leather jacket and put his hand on the door frame, hesitating. He wanted her to say something, to tell him that everything was ok and that she loved him. But inside, he knew he'd already done too much damage and there was no going back.

Unable to risk even a glance back at her, he only managed to speak once more before he left, his
voice cracking in pain.

"I love you, mo chridhe."

SARAH

I felt numb, hollow. He was willing to give me up for what? To be a vigilante and take out the man who hurt me? While a part of me loved the fact that he would do that, the logical side of me knew that the risk was too great. I didn't move from my seat on the couch for a long time, not until I heard a soft knock at the door.

I felt like I was wading through a bog as I walked to the door. I don't know what my expression is.
Looked like it, but when Isla saw me standing there, her smile faded and she immediately hugged me close.

"Oh darlin', come here!"

The warmth of her embrace broke the dam that had been holding back my tears, and I sobbed in
her arms. We stood like that for a moment, her gently comforting me while I cried, before she led me to a chair at the dining table and went into the kitchen to make me a cup of tea.

"Colin told me what the boys were thinkin', and while I'm not surprised that they want to hunt this bastard down, the fact that they're actually doin' it? That wasn't expected, for sure. When Li called me, he sounded... well, broken. I haven't heard him like that in a long time."

I could tell that Isla was using the tea as a way to keep herself distracted and occupied while she
talked. She was obviously upset and worried, but was trying to sound sure. I still couldn't think of any
words to say, so I just sat there and let her keep rambling.

"I know he means well by all this, Sarah. He loves you and he's trying to do the right thing. He just doesn't know what the right thing is, so he's doing what he knows to do, and he's so fuckin' stubborn that he can't turn himself around from it. And those lads of his... I love them, ya know, but they're just as stubborn as Li is. They'd follow him off a fuckin' cliff, I'd think. Arseholes, the lot of 'em! But bless 'em, they mean well."

She sat at the table with me while the kettle heated up and took my hand. "It's going to be ok,
darlin'."

I shook my head. "I don't think so, Isla. Even if they don't get caught, Liam basically told me he
would pick doing this over me. He's willing to let me go; all he wants to do is take Mickey out, no matter how I feel about it."

Isla sat with this information for a moment, gathering her thoughts before she spoke. "What you
need to understand about Liam... he's been broken since he was a boy. The things he went through
twisted his understanding of what it means to be a protector. He has always taken care of those around
him, fighting for the underdog in school, fallin' for the most broken women because he thinks he can save them. And his life has always had violence at the core o' it. Even when it wasn't his choice or his doin'. And now that he's found you, he's doin' the only thing he thinks he can do. It's asinine, but it's who he is, if you can find a bit o' grace for him."

"I get that he's trying to do the right thing, Isla. But to be willing to lose me over it? Do I mean
anything to him? It feels like his revenge, even on my behalf, is more important to him than I am!"

Isla nodded sympathetically. "I can see how it feels that way, love. But let me tell ya, that man
does love you. And I guarantee you, the thought that he might lose you for choosing this path, which in
his mind is the only path he has to look out for you, is killin' him. But your safety means more to him
than his own feelings, so he's moving forward with it, no matter what."

I clutched at the pendant around my neck, remembering the day he gave it to me. Liam, my strong warrior who would do anything for me, including giving me up if it meant I was out of harm's way.

I looked at Isla. "And what am I supposed to do if... if they go through with this plan? How can I look at him in the same way if he's done something like this? I love him, but this is something that could affect him for the rest of his life."

"Aye, it could. For better or worse, he won't be the same after this. I don't have an answer for you, except to say that at his core, Liam is a good man. He may not always make the right decisions, but he means well. If this whole thing makes you see him differently, I can understand, but I would say you need to really think about the risks he's taking for you. This isn't just a bar fight because some eejit made a pass at you. This is getting revenge on a man who almost killed you and threatened to come back and finish the job."

I looked down at my hands while she continued.

"Liam isn't making this decision lightly. He's doing this because of his need to take care of you.

He's prepared to face any consequences that come his way because of how much he adores you. And

whether he's doin' right or wrong, you can't forget that he's doin' it all for you."

I looked up at her serious expression. She was balancing on that fine line of admonishing me and giving advice, trying to help me see the depth of the situation, and I was truly grateful to her. She was right. Regardless of what choice he was making, he was doing it for me. I couldn't fault him for loving me enough to go to these lengths, not when I'd always hoped for someone who would do just that. I had to trust that he would still be himself, still be my Liam, when it was all said and done.

LIAM

When Liam arrived on his doorstep, Declan didn't ask for or need an explanation. He knew Liam well enough to guess at what had happened. Sarah had likely tried to talk him out of this plan, and he had been too stubborn to give up. And before they could argue more or he could say something he truly regretted, Liam had come here to get some space.

The two friends sat in silence, the TV playing in the background, until Declan went to bed. Liam sat on the couch, brooding. He hated himself for causing the pain he'd seen in Sarah's face. He wanted to go back home and assure her that he would never let her go, that everything was going to be ok... but he couldn't give up on his idea that this was the only way he could keep her safe. These thoughts rolled around in his mind like a summer thunderstorm until sleep finally claimed him just as the sun was breaking over the horizon.

There wasn't much time for them to discuss things the next day when they finally woke up. Murph and Freddy arrived just before noon, and they packed into Murph's van with Liam in the front, Declan and Freddy in the back. No one spoke; the tension was too great for words. Liam was thinking over his conversation with Sarah earlier, and the things his brother had said last week. There was a small voice in the back of his mind that said they were right; this would change him. But his anger and protective instinct were drowning out that voice, pushing it away into the depths of his brain.

It was a quarter to 9 pm when they parked at the edge of the back alley behind The Factory Floor.
Murph turned the lights off and killed the engine. There was only one street light that barely illuminated the brick walls of the club and the building next to it, and one small light bulb above the club's back door. Plenty of shadows to conceal them as they waited for Declan's friend Luke, who had agreed to be inside the club to pretend to be friendly with Mickey in order to talk him into going out the back for a smoke between sets.

One by one, they stepped out of the van and found places to stand on either side of the door, just out of sight. The minutes stretched by, feeling like hours, as Liam kept checking his watch. Finally, they heard someone laughing, and the door to the club suddenly opened.

Mickey began lighting his smoke before the door had even shut behind him and Luke. The smell of alcohol and cheap cologne wafted around him as he stretched his tall, thin frame. He was about 6ft, lean and muscular, like a runner. Liam had barely remembered him from that one night at karaoke, but as soon as he saw the man laughing at something Luke was saying, he immediately knew this was the right guy.

"That's him," he whispered softly, remembering how Mickey had tried to put his arm around Sarah.

Liam stepped out from the shadows and began walking towards the doorway. "Mickey?" he asked, trying to stop his voice from shaking with anger.

"Yeah, what's it to you?" Mickey asked warily, not noticing how Luke stepped behind him to
block him from going back through the door into the safety of the club.

"Oh, I have a message for you, from someone you may know."

Mickey frowned. "And who's that, mate?"

Liam stopped right in front of Mickey and gave him a wicked look. "Her name is Sarah."

Realization and recognition dawned on Mickey's face. "Oh... I uh... I was just having a bit of fun, ya know how it is. Them little girls like to play games. They're teases, all of 'em."

Liam felt his rage bubble up in his chest, and he forced himself to stay still. "She's not a tease."

Mickey threw his cigarette on the ground, trying to act casual. "Course she is, all women are. Act like they want you till you show interest, then pretend they changed their minds. It's all a joke. Sometimes you just have to show 'em. Teach a lesson, so to speak."

Declan, Murph, and Freddy stepped from either side to join Liam and surround Mickey. Liam
reached up and grabbed the front of Mickey's hoodie. "And you

like teaching lessons, do ya?"

"Hold on, mate! It was nothing, she was just a stupid slag. What's you're problem?" Mickey raised one hand up in surprise, but the other slid down to the pocket on his hoodie.

Liam leaned in close, "My problem is you. And she isn't nothing... she's MY WOMAN!" he roared. His fist connected with Mickey's jaw in a flash, knocking him back against Luke, who held him in place as his knees buckled. Declan and Murph started to reach for him, but before they could get a grip on his arms, Mickey twisted out of Luke's grasp and pulled a knife out of his pocket, waving it frantically through the air in their direction in an attempt to fend them off.

Shaking in his panic, he turned to Liam. "You want to fight me over her? That stupid little whore worth you getting cut for? I didn't even get a taste of her, but I'll take your word for it. If she's got you this worked up, she must be a fun little shag. Guess I'll have to try again!" he said with false bravado.

Liam growled in a blind rage and tackled Mickey to the ground. They rolled away from the door, struggling and throwing punches until the boys pulled them apart and got hold of Mickey's arms. Liam stood slowly, a cut above his eye, and his hand holding his side. A spot of bright red blood slowly started to seep through his shirt.

"Jesus, Li!" Declan rushed to him while the other three men held Mickey in place. "How bad is
It?"

Liam waved him away. "It's just a scratch, I'm fine!" He stepped toward Mickey menacingly. "You will never, EVER, go near my Sarah again. Do you understand me? As a matter of fact, I'm going to make sure you never go near any woman again."

His fists landed over and over again, into Mickey's ribs, stomach, face. Liam stopped feeling the
pain in his knuckles and just enjoyed seeing them connect with his prey. The only sound was the impact
of skin on skin, his fist hitting their mark. Each time an image of Sarah's bruised body lying on the concrete fueled his anger

further. Liam watched as Mickey's face began to distort until it was almost
unrecognizable.

Finally, he stopped and caught his breath. Mickey hung limply between Murph and Freddy,
swollen and bleeding but somehow still conscious. He looked on in horror as he watched Liam bend over to pick up the knife that had been dropped on the ground during their earlier struggle.

"I think this," Liam held up the knife, "is a fitting way for you to learn, since you're so keen on
lessons... But I'm not going to make it too quick. First things first... you're going to lose a few key body
parts. Just to make sure that you understand the consequences of hurting women. You need to know that... before you die."

Mickey's eyes grew wide. Liam watched as this poor excuse of a man began to beg for them to
show him mercy. How the hell did he think he deserved any mercy after all the things he had done? He
was nothing more than a predator, an animal, leaving a trail of women in his wake.

"You'd choose this over me?"

Sarah's voice broke through his thoughts, making him stop short, the knife still pointed in Mickey's direction. Her grief-stricken face filled his mind as he replayed that memory again and again.

Looking up at Declan quickly, he let his unspoken question flow between them. Declan nodded his head subtly, acknowledging Liam's hesitation and wordlessly telling him that he needed to stop. He
handed Mickey's limp arm to Luke and walked over to his friend.

"Brother, let's think about this. Is this really what you want? You know I've got your back, no matter what. But this is it, this is the moment you choose right or left. Whichever way you choose, you have to be sure because there's no going back."

Liam's shoulders heaved with each aching breath. "How can I just stop now? This sick fuck deserves this and more!"

"Aye, he does," Declan agreed. "But is it you who needs to deliver the punishment? What will that do to you, Liam? To Sarah?"

Remembering the pain in her eyes when she asked if he would take things this far, even if it meant losing her. A sob tore from his chest.

"AAHHHH!!" His guttural cry cut through the night. He fell to his knees, grabbing his side where the knife had pierced his skin. Declan put a hand on his shoulder as he broke down, dropping the knife to the ground.

Luke stared at him in anger. "Are ye fuckin' kidding me? You're just going to let him go? After
What he did to your woman, to my sister?"

Liam shook his head in defeat. "I can't do it, I can't let myself go there, Luke."

Rage filled Luke's eyes. "Well, if you can't do it, I will!" He jumped forward to grab the knife and turn back to Mickey. In a surge of energy fueled by pure terror, Mickey wrenched free of the boys' grasp and ran toward the street.

"Get him!" Liam called, knowing they couldn't risk letting him leave the alley.

The men all began to run after Mickey, but the frightened DJ was already several meters ahead of them. He glanced back their way to see how close they were and didn't look in front of him as he ran off the curb and tripped into the street.

Liam stopped short just before he left the shadows of the alleyway and watched in grim
fascination as the oncoming bus crunched into Mickey's body, dragging him along the street in a bloody mess. He could hear screams from people on the bus and across the street as Mickey was turned into nothing but a smear on the pavement. His blood seemed to spray everywhere like a red rain, even
reaching into the alley to splatter across Liam's face and chest.

There were shouts about calling an ambulance, but Liam could see there was no point. Mickey was gone. One of his blood-soaked trainers had somehow ended up on the sidewalk, thrown from the impact. Without looking too closely, Liam thought he noticed that there might have still been a foot inside the shoe.

Before anyone could spot them watching from the shadows, he and his friends turned to run back to the van. None of them broke the silence; they were all too stunned for words. Luke directed them to his house so they could clean up.

As they sat around Luke's table later, Declan quietly cleaned Liam's wound while Murph and Freddy sipped on bottles of lager. Luke was pacing the kitchen, fuming.

"What the fuck, Liam? You were going to let him go? And after all that, a bus took him out? That bastard got off easy, if you ask me!"

Liam glanced up and saw a faint smile on Declan's face. "Dec..." was all he could say.

Declan nodded. "Aye, you did good. I know how you were fighting with yerself, I could see it. But you made the right choice. I'm proud of you, brother." He finished putting the bandage on Liam's waist and handed him an ale. "Sarah will be proud of you too."

Liam was shaking from the adrenaline and relief that it was over. He was frightened of how close he had come to going over the edge, crossing a line that he could never come back from. He still knew that it would have been worth it for Sarah, but knowing that he could go back to her with his hands clean gave him solace.

He looked down at his broken and bleeding knuckles. Well, his hands were almost clean. The
Thought broke through the tension in his mind, and he couldn't help but laugh.

SARAH

I couldn't sit still waiting on news from Liam. Isla was still with me, getting slightly annoyed by
my pacing, but I could tell she was trying to be patient with me. Cara had been calling every hour asking if we'd heard anything yet, but each time all I could do was let her down with a sigh. Around 3 am, I finally gave in to my exhaustion and stress, passing out on the couch.

The next thing I knew, Isla was gently shaking me awake. "They're back." She whispered.

I jumped up, noticing that the sun was just starting to light up the sky. I didn't bother with a coat or shoes. I just ran to the door and flung it open. Declan was leaning against the front of his truck while Liam was slowly climbing out of the passenger door, and I could see a huge bloodstain on his shirt. He looked up at me standing in the doorway, and his eyes looked lost and searching, as if he were trying to figure out whether or not I was going to turn and run from him.

In that moment, my mind was made up. I did run... directly to the man I love.

I flung myself into him, wrapping my arms and legs around him and pushing him against the truck. I kissed him with all the love I had in my soul, barely registering the painful grunt he made.

"Careful, lass, you'll undo all the work I did getting him to stop leaking all over my truck." Declan chuckled.

I jumped to the ground and looked more closely at Liam's shirt. "You're hurt?"

He was just staring at me, like he thought I might have been a hallucination. "It... It's nothing. You stayed..."

I reached up to put a hand on his cheek. "Of course I stayed. I love you, Liam!"

He held me at arm's length and studied my face. "But... but you don't know what happened."

"It doesn't matter. Whatever you did tonight, I know you did it for me. Anything else that happens
from here on out, we'll deal with. Together. I choose you, Liam.

My Liam."

Liam's eyes filled with tears, and he suddenly fell to his knees, wrapping his arms around my waist as he cried in relief. I stroked his hair and gave Declan a questioning look.

"Is Mickey... is he gone?" I asked.

Declan nodded solemnly. "Aye. But not by Liam's hand." He gave me a meaningful smile. "You'd be proud of our boy, Sarah. Gave Mickey a good beating, but stopped himself at the end."

I knelt down to meet Liam's gaze. "You didn't do it?"

He shook his head. "Naw, I couldn't. I wanted to. I knew he deserved it. But right when I was about to put an end to him, I heard you. I heard your voice, asking me if I would choose that over you. Mo chridhe, I will never choose anything over you!"

He pulled me close and we cried together. I clung to him, overwhelmed by what he had said. We had found each other under insane circumstances, and through everything, we had chosen each other regardless of the world around us. We stayed there in each other's arms for a moment before I realized something Declan had said.

"Wait, you said Mickey was gone. If you didn't... if it wasn't you, how?"

Declan laughed as he reached down to help us both back to our feet. "Would ya believe it? Bastard got hit by a bus!"

I looked back and forth between them, shocked. "A bus?"

Liam could only nod, but Declan was still cackling. "You should have seen it, lass... Ran away from us and right into the path of a bus. Sprayed him all over the pavement, like something out of an action movie. Never seen anything like it!"

Before I could even think of a way to respond to that, a car pulled up behind Declan's truck. Colin jumped out with his medical bag and ran to us.

"Isla told me you were back. What happened? Are ya alright?" He questioned, eyeing Liam's bloodstained shirt.

"Aye, brother," Liam replied. "Everything is ok. Although it's good that you're here, I need a few stitches, I'm afraid."

We all went into the house, and while Colin was stitching Liam's side, I held his hand as he told us everything that had happened that night. I flinched when he told me about the things Mickey had said, and I'll admit, there was a part of me that was happy to hear about the beating Liam had given him. But I was even more grateful when he told us about how he had stopped himself from ending Mickey's life. I had already known that if he had gone through with it, I was staying by his side. But knowing that he kept himself from going to such extremes made my heart swell with pride.

The sun was shining brightly overhead by the time everyone left. I curled up against Liam's uninjured side and we just sat in a comfortable silence until a sudden thought made me giggle.

"And just what is so funny, Princess?"

I shrugged playfully. "I was just thinking what a pair we make, all our bruises and bandages. We're quite the couple with our matching wounds!"

He looked at me like I'd lost my mind for a moment before joining in my laughter. "Aye, that we do, love."

The exhaustion and stress of the night finally caught up to us, and we made our way to the bedroom. Liam helped me get my shirt up over my head, and I helped him tug his jeans off his legs so he wouldn't pull his stitches. We crawled into bed, our arms and legs entwined, and fell into a peaceful, contented sleep.

DECLAN

Liam was fidgeting with his braid, complaining that it didn't look right. I cuffed him on the back of the head.

"Stop acting like an old woman. Sarah isn't going to care if your hair isn't perfect!"

He nodded but then began to tug at the chain on his sporran. I punched him in the shoulder.

"If you don't stop messing around and worrying, the next punch is going straight to your face. Then you'll have to face Sarah with a black eye. Is that what you want?"

He smiled ruefully. "No."

I handed him a glass of champagne and nodded. "Good. Jesus, brother, you've got to relax. It's not like she's going to say no."

He looked up sharply, as if he hadn't even thought of that. "Say no? Do you think she might?"

"Ah, Christ... of course she won't say no. Liam, that woman has put up with more than enough from you in the last year. If she were going to run away from you, she would have done it long ago. Just take a breath and calm yerself!"

He nodded again nervously and took a swig from the champagne flute. I straightened his tie and looked him in the eye.

"Are you ready?"

Liam took a shuddered breath. "Aye. Let's go."

I couldn't remember a time when I'd seen him this nervous. We walked outside and towards the Loch, where everyone was waiting. Murph and Freddy were already in their place at the front. I gave Mrs. MacKay a kiss on the cheek as we passed by her seat, and I noticed that she was already crying.

Jesus, these MacKays are an emotional lot, I thought affectionately. Truth be told, I was fighting my own emotions today, but I wouldn't admit that to anyone.

We took our place on the dais, set against Loch Ness and the warm colors of the setting sun. Liam's hands were shaking as we waited for the music to start. I put my hand on his shoulder.

"You've got this, Liam."

He didn't reply, just kept his gaze on the aisle in front of us. Soon, the sound of violins began, signaling the beginning of the ceremony. Cara was first, her light blue dress billowing in the gentle breeze, and her eyes shone with unshed tears.

Fucking hell, was everyone going to be crying today?

Isla and Aislin took their turns next, in matching blue dresses. Isla was glowing, holding her bouquet in front of her enormous pregnancy bump. I smiled at the thought of a new little one joining this unique family of ours. Oh, the things I would teach that kid!

The music shifted into a peaceful, instrumental version of Wild Mountain Thyme. When Colin and Sarah came into view, I heard Liam sniff. He wasn't even trying to fight the tears as he watched his bride walk toward him. I put my arm around his neck and whispered an encouraging word in his ear.

"You're one lucky bastard, brother! And you deserve all the happiness in the world!"

Sarah's lacy dress moved around her with an ethereal flow, almost otherworldly, as if she were an actual fae. The crown of flowers in her hair only added to the illusion, and I honestly don't think I'd ever seen her smile that wide. Colin passed her hand to Liam, who helped her step onto the platform with us.

As I listened to them vow to love each other for all eternity and call each other out if they got out of line, I laughed along with the rest of the crowd, but a dull ache filled my chest. I couldn't help but remember when I had this kind of love, standing where Liam was now and professing my unending devotion to my bride. Losing her had torn a hole in my soul that never fully healed.

I shook my head to clear away the memories and tried to stay focused on my friends in front of me. When they kissed for the first time as husband and wife, I whistled loudly and cheered along with the other guests. I laughed as Liam picked Sarah up into his arms and carried her down the aisle.

We all danced the night away under the soft light of the outdoor lanterns and candles. Isla was trying her best to twerk, but her belly was getting in her way, much to Colin's amusement. I stole Sarah away from Liam for a dance of my own, spinning her around the floor.

"I'm glad you're officially part of the family, lass. 'Bout time someone made an honest man outta Liam!"

Hugging me affectionately, she smiled at me in a way that pierced my heart. "Thank you, Declan. It's an honor to be a part of this family. You've all done so much for me."

"Ach, the honor is all ours. You're good for him. I've never seen him this happy. But if he ever gets to be too much of an arsehole, you just call me. I'll come set him straight."

She laughed. "Deal!"

I stayed until Liam and Sarah left for their honeymoon, a trip to New Zealand of all places. When I asked Liam why they chose New Zealand, he just shrugged.

"Sarah wants to see the Shire!"

After they left, everyone else stayed to keep the party going and the beer flowing, but I quietly tried to make an escape. Isla caught me, however, and took my hand in hers.

"Where do ye think yer going?"

I sighed. "I just needed a break from all the dancing. I got tired of showing everyone up with my wicked skills."

She grinned. "I see... I'm glad it's not because you're trying to get away to be by yerself." She gave me a knowing look, pulling me toward one of the benches at the edge of the crowd.

"Listen, sis, you need to quit reading my mind like that."

Shrugging, she just waved my comment away. "When you stop trying to get away with shite like this, I'll stop reading your mind. Now, tell me the truth. Why were you leaving?"

"I guess... I just needed to clear my head. You know I'm thrilled for Li and Sarah, and I was proud to stand up with him today. It just..."

"Brings back memories?" Isla said softly.

"Aye."

She patted my hand. "I understand, Dec. Anyone would. But we're your family. If you can't talk to us and lean on us when you need support, then what good are we? Every single person over there, no matter how drunk they might be at the moment, knows exactly why you're feelin' this way. But we're all here for you. Don't hid yerself away."

I looked up towards the laughing crowd, still celebrating, and I could see all the love everyone shared for each other. I might not be related by blood, but these crazy eejits were my family. I knew they'd do anything for me, and I for them.

I gave Isla a sly grin and helped pull her to her feet. "Alright, you've won. I'll come back to the party. But you have a give me another dance."

"Of course!" She smiled, happy that she'd succeeded in changing my mind.

I frowned. "Just promise me something?"

"Anything, Dec, what is it?"

"This time, don't whack me with that belly of yours?"

She smacked me on the back of the head hard enough that my teeth rattled, but she laughed and we walked arm in arm back to the dance floor.

ACKNOWLEDGEMENTS

Writing has been a lifelong dream of mine, and it's been a long road to finally get here. I wanted to take a moment and thank the people who have inspired and encouraged me along the way.

To Anna: My best friend since birth, my sister. You have always been there for me and helped me keep my head above water more times than I can count. You've seen me through my darkest moments and shared in my greatest joys. Thank you for always believing in me. I love you!

To Lajah: You've always had my back and looked out for me, encouraging me and giving me the hard truth when I needed it. For five years, you've been a constant source of encouragement, laughter, and support. I'm so incredibly grateful to have you in my life. ILYF!

To David: You've been a true friend, finding ways to make me smile, encourage me, and inspire me at the exact moments I needed it the most. Are you a mind-reader? You are such an unbelievably special person, and I hope you realize that! Thank you for everything!

To Sandi, my long-distance sister for over 20 years! You've seen me through the good, the bad, and the ugly times of my life and have always stood by my side. I'll never be able to repay you for all the love and support you've given me. PS, give Dom a hug from me!

To Viktor: My brother, you have done more for me than I can say. You've been a constant source of support, given the best advice, and introduced me to the Land of Enchantment. Even if you can't forget certain knee-related stories, I'm so glad you're in my life, and I'm proud to be your sister!

To Mom: Thank you! You are the reason I am the woman I am today. I miss you every day!

There are so many other people, I could write 50 pages of names. To everyone who encouraged me, asked to read my book, and gave me the confidence to keep going – I love you all! This book is for all of you!

S. E. Walker

ABOUT THE AUTHOR

S. E. Walker

Hi, I'm S. E. Walker—writer, dreamer, and lifelong lover of stories that blur the line between heartbreak and healing. I write from my soul, often drawing on personal experiences, strange dreams, and the quiet power of determination.

Originally from the Midwest and now enjoying life beneath the Sandia Mountains of New Mexico, I spend my nights working remotely and my days writing, building fictional towns, and drinking too much coffee. Whether it's an unexpected romance, a haunted espresso machine, or a 500lb hell-hound, my stories always come with a little grit, a little magic, and a lot of heart.

I believe stories can save us—and for me, they already have.

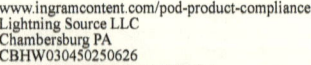